GRIMMISH

Whispers of Pain

Michael Winkler

GRIMMISH

224 pp. Toronto: Coach House Books

978 1 55245 466 4

I recently made a ponderously slow rereading of the preferred English version of the famous work written in Portuguese by Bernardo Soares, a heteronym of Fernando Pessoa. In one of his footnotes to *The Book of Disquiet* translator Richard Zenith provides an alternative translation for a phrase he has chosen to use in the text. The wording that appears in Zenith's English version of the book is 'thereby shoving it up against the wall.' The alternative he offers is 'thereby letting it flow like a river, the slave of its own bed.' The gap between these options is oceanic. The translator doubtless agonized over the best possible rendition of the original Portuguese, but what is the English-language reader left with? A pasty simulacra of whatever Soares/Pessoa intended. A whisper of a whisper of a whisper.

Pessoa's peculiar meisterwork is one of the disparate sources ransacked by Michael Winkler in *Grimmish*. A book ostensibly about the hapless Italian-American boxer Joe Grim's visit to Australia in 1908–09, *Grimmish* spirals into knottier regions including motivations behind the author's attraction to the Grim story, problems of fictionalized history, how a contemporary writer handles gap-riddled historical narratives, and most of all the rich realm of pain.

Overarching Winkler's peregrinations is the question of authenticity, and the impossibility that this presentation of Grim will bear much or any connection to the flesh-and-blood fighter Joe Grim. How pale is this simulacrum? How faint the whisper?

There is no narrative arc, close to zero love interest, skittish occasional action, incident rather than plot, and a narrator who is intermittently compelling but prevaricates and self-deludes like a broody prince at Elsinore. Winkler lards proceedings with asides that are intermittently useful and sometimes distracting. He revels in the construction of deliberately rickety storytelling structures, and enjoys a little too much the stunt of toppling his mouthpieces into knowingly unrealistic dialogue. Is anything profound said about Australia, or about manhood, or about individuals who choose a little-travelled path, and that ostensibly strange life choices can provide an existence as valid as any other? Yes, conceivably. Has the pain theme been wrung for every last drop? Probably, and possibly a few too many drops more.

It is not impossible that the formal conceit employed here, explicated by the author as 'an exploded non-fiction novel,' may be a model that will repay further future exploration. Winkler wins points for his evident devotion to a narrow and seemingly unpromising strip of subject matter. He makes a convincing case for Grim as an exceptional creature, and the evocation of early twentieth-century pugilism is solid. The inclusion of extracts from contemporary newspaper accounts lends context and delivers some linguistic delights, although less tenacious readers may find they impede progress.

Whether a profitable balance between Grim's story, metafictional meddling, Winkler's ruminations on pain, and jocose and fanciful scads of fiction has been achieved is moot. The suspicion lurks that Winkler failed to unearth sufficient documentary material in the research phase to sustain a conventional non-fiction treatment, and his decision to ameliorate this shortfall with stylistic shenanigans will not be to every taste. Additionally, the sustained depiction of physical violence is likely to alienate some, while others may weary of the defiant wallowing in the sludge of masculinity. The grand total of female characters in *Grimmish*? One.

Convinced of the artificiality of conventional fiction, Winkler knots himself tighter than a fishing fly attempting to find new ways to convey the Grim story. It is passing strange that the author seems to be commenting on the artificiality of the conventional novel at a time when storytelling, in all of its modalities, has never been more variegated and sophisticated. However, there are some novel touches, including the inclusion of a review at the beginning of the book, and the crazy paving of the narrative approach could be judged to make perfect sense (and/or appropriate non-sense) within the context of the subject matter. There is likely to be a readership, however small, that enjoys what Winkler is attempting to do, and finds within these covers something sincere and worthwhile. Sometimes it is a question of timing, the happenstance of the right reader meeting the right book at the right time.

In an era of post-post-modernism, when authenticity is regarded in some quarters as the only valid currency and in others as an irrelevancy, Winkler seems to be arguing for feelings above facts, as long as the feelings are his own. Hence, we are given several incursions through the fourth wall that beg to be parsed as radical authorial honesty, demystifying the process by which he has chosen to fictionalize the many parts of Grim's Australian adventure that are undocumented and must remain unknown. An alternative interpretation registers it as recursive self-indulgence bolstering the tendency to obfuscate, as if clarity itself was something from which to flee, as dangerous as the hooks and crosses of a heavyweight boxer.

More than a century after Grim left Australian shores, is it possible to frame his endeavours as heroic in their enactment of extreme physical humility? Can anything profound be drawn from an individual so singular, involved in activities so barbarous? Would any two biographical translations arrive at any agreement on who he was and what went on and why? Can we be comfortable that trying to account for Grim must always resolve into desperate whispering in shadows?

It is difficult to ascertain. Pessoa might have had an answer, even if Bernardo Soares did not. Perhaps it just comes down to the old joke: Two anarchists are making Molotov cocktails. One says, 'So mate, who do we throw them at?' The other replies, 'What are you, some kind of fucking intellectual?' ▪

GRIMMISH

MICHAEL WINKLER

COACH HOUSE BOOKS, TORONTO

LIBRARY AND ARCHIVES CANADA CATALOGUING IN PUBLICATION

Title: Grimmish / Michael Winkler.
Names: Winkler, Michael, 1966- author.
Identifiers: Canadiana (print) 2023013291X | Canadiana (ebook) 20230132944 | ISBN 9781552454664 (softcover) | ISBN 9781770567658 (EPUB) | ISBN 9781770567665 (PDF)
Classification: LCC PR9619.4.W56 G75 2023 | DDC 823/.92—dc23

Grimmish is available as an ebook: ISBN 978 1 77056 765 8 (EPUB), ISBN 978 1 77056 766 5 (PDF)

Purchase of the print version of this book entitles you to a free digital copy. To claim your ebook of this title, please email sales@chbooks.com with proof of purchase. (Coach House Books reserves the right to terminate the free digital download offer at any time.)

For Z, and for J

Nurse, where are we going?
– To the morgue.
But I haven't died yet.
– Well, we haven't arrived yet.

1.

Red of slit eye. Red of slashed eyelid. Red of tongue sliced this way and that. Red of screaming echoes in cudgelled ears. Red of gashed nose. Red of welt and rent and tear. Red of broken gum and tooth and mouth. Red of leering gaping eyebrow. Red of flayed forehead. Red of intracranial bleeding. Red of torn nostril. Red of smacked cheek. Red of swollen jaw. Red of ripped lobe. Red the river from roaring red core spewing redly through red-slapped mouth. Red mask. Red veil. Red the abuse, abuse.

2.

My uncle Michael was not in good health. This was not unexpected. He was not in fact my uncle, but my great-great or possibly great-great-great-great, and there was even wobbliness about whether he was a blood relative or just someone who had been around the place for so long he passed as family. I did not know his age, but he was exceptionally old. And now he was poorly, apparently.

His room reminded me always of the bow wake of an ocean liner. A narrow strip of worn carpet led from the door to the armchair where he sat, slept, surveyed. On either side were titanic walls of paper. Books, magazines, newspapers, letters. The mounds never seemed to slip or alter, but there was the ever-present threat that one day a manual on farm mechanics from 1927, say, might be knocked loose and then the whole shebang would shift and slide, a concatenation of paper movement ending with my uncle, who was probably not my uncle, ending his life submerged beneath his own paper history.

I closed the door behind me, closed out the bright day. Adjusted as always to the smell. Rotting paper, musty paper, paper more dust than paper. Well, he said, the dark wings are flapping today.

He always wanted to talk – endlessly, actually – which was why I avoided visiting, usually. But on this day he wanted to postpone the pleasure. Come back tomorrow, he said. That won't be easy, I said, trying to remember my schedule, remembering that it was blank, but not wanting to make this effort all over. I've never told you about Grim, he said, and I need to prepare. I asked who or what that was. Joe Grim, he said. I'm not the best today, and I've got reading to do. You look him up, too. Get the gist, then come and see me tomorrow. Bring sherry.

3.

I did as I was told. And found: singular, astounding Joe Grim, more forgotten than remembered. Joe Grim, pain artiste. Born Saverio Giannone on or about 16 March 1881 in Avellino, Campania, Italy. Migrated to the U.S.A. when he was ten. Worked as a shoeshine boy in Philadelphia, started frequenting boxing gyms as a sparring partner, then commenced fighting as a professional in 1899. In his first three years he had seventy-eight recorded bouts and won thirty-one of them. Then he stepped up in class, fought greats and near-greats like Philadelphia Jack O'Brien, Joe Walcott, Dixie Kid, and Peter Maher. A fight against Bob Fitzsimmons in 1903 seemed to set him on a different course. He lost, but attracted wide attention for his ability to endure six rounds with the former world champion. After that he combatted immortals like Jack Johnson and Joe Gans and countless lesser lights, and his contests changed in a profound sense, becoming not about winning or losing, but hinging on whether or not he could endure the punishment meted out. And on that score he invariably triumphed. Fitzsimmons said he was the hardest proposition to knock out that he ever met. Johnson said, I just don't believe that man is made of flesh and blood. Grim became a spectacle rather than a fighter, but he was popular and he made a living.

In 1908 he journeyed to Australia and stayed in the country for about a year and a half. His first fight on Australian soil[1] was

---

1   BoxRec is the Domesday Book of pugilism. Accuracy is its watchword. It listed Joe Grim's first Australian fight as taking place on 10 June 1908 in Sydney against a man simply called Devaney. Given BoxRec's authority, I accepted this as fact and squandered acres of research time trying to discover more about the contest. Except that it never happened. Grim did not arrive in Australia until several months after that date.

versus George Stirling, known delightfully as the Cobar Chicken. Joe swung into the limelight, according to the *Sydney Sportsman*, a full balloon of style. He burst upon the eyes of the multitude like 'Julia' Caesar preparing for the bath. He wore a gorgeous dressing gown, said to have been borrowed from Mrs. Farrell. He did a cakewalk round the ring several times, with the idea of scaring Stirling before the battle commenced. Grim looked like a circus clown suddenly given a half holiday, or else a Japanese mikado just tripping to his wedding. *Referee* contributes the observation that he grabbed an imaginary dance partner for a giant stride waltz that quite put the mass of onlooking men off its balance. That publication applauded the setting, a roomy, roofless structure, within which one could stretch one's limbs, puff away at one's pipe with freedom, and breathe pure God-given atmosphere while gazing at the starlit dome above. *Referee* put the crowd at three thousand and claimed Grim disrobed to disclose as fair a round belly as ever a junior friar boasted, and little rolls of fat that

---

Where did the phantom fight come from? His international reputation, and perhaps the stir that he caused among local fans, meant a battling Sydney lightweight started calling himself Joe Grim II, and on 15 June 1909 (just over a year after the erroneous fight supposedly occurred) this upstart fought Horace Devaney in Sydney. Presumably that is where the confusion arose. I alerted BoxRec, and within a day the official record was altered. I also deposed that there were three more fights Grim undertook on his Australian tour that were not part of the official record. I had uncovered:

- 12 February 1909 vs. Sid Russell, Melbourne Athletic Club – Grim lost, Pts
- 9 March 1909 vs. Tom Fennessey, Her Majesty's Theatre, Ballarat – Grim lost, Pts
- 6 May 1909 vs. Bob Fraser, Theatre Royal, Perth – Draw

Getting the BoxRec listing changed felt like I had bent history the way a sideshow strongman bends an iron poker. The past, we know, is malleable, and representations of what has transpired can only ever be partial, subjective, contestable – but changing the international record books, the official history of the sport, with a single email felt odd.

bulged over his waistband, although the brawniness of his right arm was also acknowledged. The *National Advocate* noted this was Grim's 348th fistic battle and had the crowd at seven thousand. The *Australian Star* thought there were three thousand to four thousand onlookers, that Grim had an unexceptional body, and enjoyed that in the ninth round after a hard scuffle Grim stopped fighting and remarked to his opponent, You thought you had me, didn't you, boy? This may have come after, as the *Sportsman* observed, Stirling bashed in one, two, three hot 'uns to the ribs. Breaking away, Grim sent a lightning right into the Cobar Chicken's tater trap. More clinches and short-arm jolts, with Grim snorting all the time like a traction engine. Stirling a clear winner on points. *National Advocate* claimed that Joe said something after the fight about bananas. The same source reported several weeks earlier that Grim, a Dago, states that the oyster and banana vendors will roll up in thousands to see him fight.

A fortnight later, Grim's second antipodean bout was against Arthur Cripps at the Gaiety Athletic Hall. Under the headline 'The Grim Joke' and the subhead 'By Cripes, He Is Walloped By Cripps,' and the sub-subhead 'Tastefully Trounced In Twenty,' the *Sportsman* writer's racial-humourist intentions are fully telegraphed with the opening gambit, which states that Da Stake-a-da-oyst gentry dug their wings into the staves of the staunch set o' small supporters, their anxiety being to see Signor Josephus Grim wipe Arthur Cripps off the earth in twenty spasms. It went the full twenty, spasms or otherwise, in which the Iron Man's lips were again gaily painted, points verdict to the local man. The *Australian Star* said any boxer would have been content to crawl away to bed after the contest but this was not so with Grim. Although sore of body, with his mouth cut and bleeding, his left eye closed and a 'mouse' on his forehead as big as a pigeon's egg, Grim seemed as fresh as when he entered the ring, and as soon as the verdict was given against him he jumped across the floor and vaulted over the ropes into the audience.

His third outing was against Jim Griffin. The *Sportsman* declaimed that it was tip-top tip-tappery that engorged the crowd numbers such as they bulged the battens of the Gaiety, a bosker house, for the grimmage[2] between Joyful Joe of Philadelphia and Genial Jim of Maoriland. Griffin invariably avoided his clumsy leads and hooked Joe to the brisket. Grim landed a right on Griffin's ribs, and gave a loud gasp of delight, which won another round. Jim kept pounding fiercely into the Iron Man's pantry. Joe grunted each time. Jim punished Joe a hatful. Once when Griffin scored downstairs, Grim stood and performed a half-second dance of derision. Hot stuff flying. The Maorilander started his left to work. Stab after stab he sent into Grim's dial. Joe's smeller began to spurt like a fountain. Suddenly the sensation of the night happened. Pressing Grim back, Griffin hooked him square on his alleged iron jaw, and, amid a wild yell that nearly split the roof, Joe went with a crash to the floor. Dazed, he rose up after a few seconds. Joe, reeling against the ropes, was dead to the world. But before Griffin could get the king hit home, the bell clanged and Joe was saved. Poor Grim then attempted to throw a handspring, but his attempt was ludicrous. He fell on the seat of his trunks. Some of the crowd cheered, others hooted. It was a great slather and whack fight. There is no gainsaying Grim's pluck and ability to take punishment. But there is a big chunk of his reputation gone now that Griffin dropped him.

---

2   The *Sydney Sportsman* perhaps intended 'scrimmage,' but 'grimmage' is felicitous.

4.

I returned to my uncle's room the next day, as directed. I wondered how much of his story would be Grim and how much would be him.[3] He said, Oh, it's you, but then before I was fully inside the paper embankments he said, Where's the sherry? I apologized and hurried off to find a bottlo and secured a two-litre flagon of McWilliam's Royal Reserve. Oh, it's you, he said, letting me back in, then creaking down the channel running through the parting in the paper Red Sea, resuming his place in the armchair. He poured a hefty belt of sherry into his teacup.

I said, So – Grim?

The most remarkable cove, he said. I'll start with the memory that bulges largest just now: the first time I ever saw him. Against Mike Williams of Ireland.

And he proceeded, like this:

Eleven days before Christmas, 1908. The Cyclorama on Victoria Parade at Eastern Hill, this curious hexagonal building originally used to exhibit massive pictures that paying customers could promenade around, but now a venue for circuses and stoushes. I was just a young fella then, but I had to see Grim. Something about his story. Something about him. Slotted into one of the cheapest seats, but there are no bad vantages in the Cyclorama, and the only impediment to vision is the fug of pipe smoke lifting above the hats of the men at ringside. I am restless, even nervous, and that surprises me. The early attractions are anodyne, four- and six-round gallops, little-known contestants plucked from market stalls or abattoirs

---

3   'People like to separate storytelling which is not fact from history which is fact. They do this so that they know what to believe and what not to believe.' Jeanette Winterson, *Oranges Are Not the Only Fruit*

around the inner suburbs. A couple of risible decisions, some quick victories, one late knockout executed with shocking violence midway through the final round. The crowd in good form, Christmas cheer abundant, summer's sap rising. I have enough money for a lager and a tram ticket home; I settle for two lagers and shanks' pony, trying to buff the edge off my nerves. I want Grim to be at his best, and I want him to astonish, and I want him to prevail (on his own terms, of course).

Mike Williams slopes to the ring, a colossus, each fist in its worn glove the size of a plucked pullet. His nose is long and straight for a pug, eyes like raisins pushed deep into dough, not a lot of scar tissue on the heavy brows. He glowers at the spectators in the close rows and stomps unhappily between the neutral corners, in and out of the resin box, scuffing his feet into the calico. The men around me are alive to Williams's reputation. One loud lad barks that four of Williams's last seven losses have been disqualifications, watch out for the dirty varmint holding and hitting, we know you were in southern Africa but it doesn't mean you're allowed to punch down south. Much laughter. I join the chatter; we cheap-seat aficionados agree Williams is no mug, but at best he's a second-runger. He was South African heavyweight champ, defended the belt four times, lost it, defended it another three times, but he falls short against the stiffest company: he won the West Australian heavyweight mantle, but was smashed unconscious challenging Bill Squires for the Australian and Empire belt. Last month he starched Sid Russell, the Baby Elephant, but that was his first win in four outings.

Conversation is halted by a whoop pursued by a collective in-breath from the crowd, because Joe Grim is sweeping to the very centre of the Cyclorama in a long, light-coloured gown. He climbs the steps, ducks under the top rope, and is already jawing. I can't make out what he says, but pockets of the crowd closest to him erupt in laughter. He shakes a fist across the ring at Williams, throws his hands in the air while shouting something to someone behind the timekeeper's table, whirls off the gown, and reveals a pair of bright blue silk shorts.

The announcer, all Brylcreem and bow-tie, clambers centre stage, lifts the microphone, and announces an INTERNATIONAL ATTRACTION pitting IRELAND VIA SOUTH AFRICA against ITALY VIA THE UNITED STATES. Mike Williams, a VERY READY thirteen stone eleven, recent contender for the Empire heavyweight honour, the pride OF all Ireland, please WELCOME. Across the ring, the DAGO THEY CAN NOT BREAK, the INDIA RUBBER MAN, the PHYSICAL FREAK AND PHENOMENON, stripped and willing at twelve stone three, indomitable JOE DA GRIM.

I move forward five rows without the attendant noticing. Now I can see Grim's long face, sloping brows, olive skin. Dark socks rolled down to just above the tops of his black ring boots. His calves are magnificent, sculptured, and he is well muscled through the thighs, but his torso carries some loose flesh. Referee Jack McGowan holds the combatants close in centre ring as he gives his instructions, then seconds out, ding ding, and it's on.

Sort of. Williams is plodding, mechanical, stumping forward with his big right fist cocked behind a slow left jab. Grim starts the round bobbing his head side to side, then seems to lose interest in that tactic and tries to swat away Williams's predictable leads. He stops some; others get through. Grim is ungainly, has no jab to speak of, but once or twice uncurls a soaring right uppercut that misses the intended target by about half a yard. The crowd pulses with laughter.

Round two is much like round one, and round three likewise. Grim becomes less interested in defence and spends increasing amounts of time stopping ponderous lead lefts with his teeth. By the fourth, Williams is blowing hard from the exertion. From my aerie I can see the frustration starting to crease the Irishman's face. A bloke in front of me cups his hands and bellows, Hey, Williams, want me to go home and get me kitchen sink? It's the only thing you haven't hit him with yet.

Grim looks lugubrious. Grouchy. He keeps throwing that ridiculous lead uppercut, and it continues to miss by a mile, and the crowd continues to hoot. Mostly the boxers wrestle. Williams wants to clinch and work Grim over with kidney punches and hard short chops to the base of the spine. Grim seeks security by wedging his head against the bigger man's shoulder, snaking an arm around his waist like a waltz partner, taking away space. From time to time Williams rears back from the hips to create a gap, then creases Grim's face with the blade of his forearm. At least twice he rakes his laces across Grim's eye sockets, drawing blood. Referee McGowan flaps about ineffectually, sensible of the lousy quality of spectacle but unable to influence its course.

I think the crowd is going to turn ugly, but I am wrong. They have decided to enjoy it as a novelty. We have seen great fighters in our town. Tonight is about something else, a boxing burlesque, and the spectators boo and giggle as if they are watching a vaudeville show at the Tiv. Grim is dropped once or twice, but of course he is India rubber, bouncing back up just in time. Williams rabbit-punches him, he twists his thumb in his eye, every dirty move. Grim is cut and bloody and sweating, blood and water in his eyes, swaying like a mizzen mast in a storm, but even though he goes down intermittently he won't stay down, and with each successive ascension to his feet the crowd yells louder.

As the eighth round ends, there is a din as Grim returns to his corner. He refuses to sit on the stool, refuses to look at or listen to his seconds, but is screaming something at a patron. Attendants move toward the row, and without premeditation I see a chance, take it, and hurry to a vacant inner circle seat, two yards from the ring apron. Williams is glowering and I hear every word of him swearing at his chief second. There is a heavy layer of sweat across his back and shoulders, and his face is murderous. I can hear Grim as well, hurling gibberish from his torn lips: ai ai, banana, bologna, Boccaccio, ee-yah. Any silly thing.

The bell is struck, so much louder from this stolen vantage, and as the contestants lurch toward each other I sneak a look at my new neighbours. On one side is a thin effete man in a pale grey trilby and a pale grey suit, with a pale grey face and lips as thin as cigarette papers. On my other side is – a John Hop. A member of the constabulary. A dirk of ice punctures my seat-stealing heart, but he doesn't even seem to see me.

The view here is so good, it is like a different event. I see the little snake of blood running down from the corner of Grim's left eye, the mush of his tattered mouth, the spit and froth on his chin. I can see an old scar on the side of Williams's leg, blotches on his back, the tide of sweat that has almost drenched his trunks. Grim is making an uncanny locomotive noise with his nose and mouth, and his square-on attack is feeble. Williams stops clinching and starts whaling some solid smacks into Grim's body. The Italian looks diminished, almost shrinking at the assault, and then he walks into a ramrod right to the point of the jaw, and goes down, and surely no man can come back from a blow as clean and hard as that. All around me people jump up, a seesaw effect with them leaping as Grim falls, mad clatter of displaced chairs, McGowan is counting, three … four … five, and then Grim is up. Impossible. Roars! Moments later, another blow smacks into Grim's face with a sound like a shovel hitting a watermelon, and he collapses again. Again the crowd rises, this time the count reaches six, and he drags himself upright to let the assault begin again, and the noise is doubling with each feat of unhuman forbearance. Grim goes down every three or four punches, clambers back up, and the crowd is laughing now, laughing because it is so preposterous one man could wear so much punishment, but Williams seems to think they are laughing at him. He is off the map, hitting with the heel of the glove, hammer-fisting, backhanding.

When the round ends, Grim is arguing with McGowan, shaking angry gestures at his corner men, babbling a soup of vowels and guttural consonants. I look at Williams; he looks humiliated. The police inspector next to me is making a grunting sound, shifting in his seat, crossing and uncrossing his arms. By the start of the tenth, Grim is bedraggled, a dirty jerky marionette. He mooches out of his corner, is whacked on the ear, and folds to the canvas for a couple of seconds, before standing up again. Williams seems to have found new energy, and there is no longer even the pretence of attack from his opponent, so he rumbles forward at Grim without risk, gulping air into his mouth, trying to find the energy and power to end the event. A hook to the body and a sickening crack across Grim's cheekbone and the smaller man concertinas again, pulls himself to hands and knees, and again regains his feet. Pandemonium in the terraced seating. The spectators seem to love this, as much as I hate it, and the smell of pipe tobacco is laced with excited sweat and the obscure male secretions produced at times of glittering violence. Grim tries to grapple his opponent, slumping against him and attempting to get an arm behind Williams's head, but his adversary responds with a short head-butt McGowan does not seem to notice, which opens another wound across Grim's brow. He is still making his locomotive noises, but there is an extra sound there, like an animal in distress, but his face shows no distress, his face a mask of indifference, scarlet and pulpy, jaw now slack open, carcass reddened and brutalized, and he stumbles from foot to foot and remains swaying either side of true vertical. For most of the long stanza Grim manages to fall forward onto Williams's chest, shorten distance, evade some of the bigger man's increasingly wild blows, absorb others, and Williams wears a face of mortification and anger and confusion and embarrassment, his arms are heavy with all the punches he has thrown, he seems confused, he has never hit a man so hard and so often and not been able to finish a fight. I see every moment of visible thought and execution as he pulls Grim's body around, positions it between himself and the referee, and drives a wicked low blow into Grim's groin. The Italian's body slumps further, but he stays standing, swaying still, weight on one foot and then the other, head hanging. Williams is dog-tired, and his punches into the purple mush of Grim's face are not ending the fight, and he looks at referee McGowan and seems torn as to whether or not he should risk yet another disqualification. He has fouled throughout the fight, hitting low, hitting behind the neck, holding and striking, and McGowan has done nothing, and the fight has not concluded, and he is exhausted, and no one seems to know what to do; an orgy of action has brought us to a point where everything seems peculiarly becalmed, and everyone bereft of ideas to solve the deadlock. Williams only knows how to hit and hurt and Grim only knows how to stand and the referee would like to be anywhere else. Williams steps back instead of forward, marshals his wind for a while, then drives back into Grim's ugly flesh, twists another big right into his face, and Grim goes down again. The crowd is ecstatic; this is the finest of sport. Apparently. McGowan is down on the canvas now, peering at Grim's face from close quarters, counting the inexorable beats toward double figures, when Grim hauls himself back onto his feet at count nine. Maybe nine and a half.

I feel a scream rising in me, and I know I cannot scream in this company, I am seeing what I came here to see, but I am sick with it, and I just don't know, and then there is a caterwaul close by and I am bumped sideways, and the John Hop has pushed past me and is up on the ring apron with his big right mitt making a horizontal chopping motion, louder uproar from crowd, and the inspector has beckoned McGowan across and speaks in his ear, and McGowan shrugs and then nods, and he waves in turn to the timekeeper's table and signals to the announcer, the busy beetle with the slick hair and the microphone, and the beetle rushes into the ring and announces LADIES and gentlemen, HER MAJESTY'S VICTORIA POLICE have stepped in and ordered this fight to be concluded. THEREFORE referee McGowan DECLARES THE WINNER to be the pride of Ireland, the African phenomenon, Mike WILLIAMS.

Hoots and commotion, the ref raises Williams's arm and I watch Williams's head fall forward, a man publicly shamed. He leaves the ring immediately. Grim stays in there, staggering around like the town drunk, smacking his own chest and roaring noises of triumph to the louder and louder crowd, screaming to the crowd that the fight should not have been stopped, spit and blood. The crowd deliriously happy. He shouts that he wants to fight Tommy Burns next, that no man on earth can knock him out, that he is the Iron Man, he will wager with any taker that no man alive can put out his lights. We are waiting for his patented handspring but it doesn't come. His face transforms in the instant he stops talking, now completely without animation, vacant, a man lifting and then lowering his mask, and he leaves the ring to resounding cheers but without making a response. Suddenly it is like the whole crowd is sharing one chuckle, there is much banter, much merriment, it is almost Christmas, it is a gorgeous early summer night, a good humoured exeunt of good fellows, off home after an evening to remember. I linger as if I have no place to go, or can't face the long walk back to my lodgings, or because I can't manage to say goodbye to it yet.

As the river of chuckling men ebbs out through the Cyclorama doors, I hurry down the short tunnel toward the dressing rooms. No one tries to stop me. I want to see his body. Need to. Maybe put my hand in his side. Metaphorically. But I choose the wrong direction and without intending I am in Williams's room, a fusty box with water-scarred plaster walls that stinks of urine and liniment. A cornerman is using the ring doctor's scalpel to slice apart the big man's gloves; Williams's hands have swollen so much the gloves cannot be removed in the normal manner. He has destroyed the bones of his hands on Grim's head. I wonder how long it will be before he can get back in the ring. If he needs a lengthy spell to let his fists repair, it will mean Grim has not only made him lose face but made him lose money as well. No one speaks to anyone, and I spin and leave the miserable environs of a man who supposedly won and looks like he has lost everything.

Grim's room is on the other side of the corridor. He is being sewn up, a neat row of catgut stitches closing the gash in one brow. He has been wiped down, leaving smears of drying blood across his brutalized face and torso. The promoter is there, and as the cut man tugs and labours at the stitches, Grim jabbers at the money man, checking his purse is intact and collecting on a side bet that Williams could not knock him out. Damn close call tonight, Joe, the promoter says. No, not even close. My money was always safe. You want me again, eh? You double the fee, I fight here next month. You saw the crowd loved Joe Grim. The promoter says yes, maybe, and thank you again. Grim says nothing, just tucks the money into his satchel and waits impatiently for the stitching to finish.

No one speaks to me here either. I grab a metal pail and fill it with warm water, then crouch below the bench Grim is sitting on and unlace his boots, remove them, roll down his socks. I use a sponge to wash his feet, sponge his legs from the knees to the ankles, feel the mahogany hardness of his calf muscles, wash the grime from between his toes. I kneel there for a long time, washing from high on his legs to the soles of his feet, then work my thumbs deep into the muscles, massaging from above to below, then wash him down again.

5.

I waited for my uncle to say more. He was in some kind of reverie. Transported. It is so utterly hard to make sense of this to you, he said, finally. Ideally it would be helpful if someone punched you over and again in the face. See how many smashes to your pretty lips you could endure before whimpering, screaming, begging, blackout, et cetera. That would provide bedrock prehension. You'd know where you were. But perhaps you can manage to get there via thought alone: try picturing a baseball bat swung with great force into your exposed ribs, under the armpit. Try to conceive of a well-aimed mallet landing erratically just above your left ear, and you with no means to stop it. Imagine these things are happening to you in front of a crowd baying like starved dogs. [4] Imagine a single vicious punch to your face, and then multiply it by a hundred or many hundred, and then think of the cheering that each punch drags from thousands of jeering onlookers. [5] Or, at least, dredge up a memory of the last time you suffered acute pain: the suddenness, the unfairness, the howling confusion, the way the blood thrashed inside your brain and nerve endings exploded like bottles in a shot-up saloon. Make these thoughts seep deep into your body until you have an actual physiological reaction from kinetic knowledge held in your meat and your bones, an irruption without end. Then we have some gesture toward understanding Grim. Then we can create a starting point. Where are you at with pain?

---

[4] 'The fight crowd is the most unreasoning, unjust, vicious, and vindictive of the audiences of sport.' W. C. Heinz, *The Fireside Book of Boxing*

[5] 'To hit or be hit in the face, to have your masculinity so nakedly tested, that was something else: visualized, yes, but still incomprehensible, a mystery. The great fighter was distant, a man to be invented and shaped by the fan's imagination.' Mark Kram, *Ghosts of Manila*

Physical pain?

Let's leave the other, please. Physical pain.

I dread it. Avoid it, hate it.

Yes, like the rest of us. All right then. The thing – you know, all history erases or at least downgrades pain. Something ameliorative about time, whether we want that or not. We can't believe the people in the history books felt pain in the way we do. And when you think of being flayed alive, or burned at the stake, or dragged behind horses, or any of that business – tongue splitting, bright hot steel in the rectum – it is a mercy. But the kingdom of pain was always there. We just cope with it less well today, probably because we visit it less often.

Okay, I said. Did you ask Grim about his pain?

I'm telling the story, he said. My story, my timing. First – you know, I clipped phrases from the local newspaper reports on his Australian fights. Made my own rough poem. You can read it left to right, top to bottom; read it back to front arse about upside down cake if you want. I found it in my files last night. It helps, though: sets a mood. He gestured toward the eastern paper pile. I uncreased the faded page he pushed across – Dada (dadum), he said – and I read aloud:

The freak fighter who is a Dago
Punch him in the slats if he wants to win
'You come and hava da fight and I showa you'
That nob is castiron
Grinning and invitingly holding his jaw up to be jolted
The crowd convulsed
Mouth looked like it had been hit with a bladder of blood
Flopped to his hams with a heavy flop
Hit with a sweep upwards from the boards and a chop from high aloft
Such laughter and excitement

Remarkable vitality of the tornado in human form
So many swings smiting vacancy
Catching the jab on his carmined lips
A fair left rip to the napper
Jolts and clinches
Jolts and clinches
A terrific right on his listener
Stood and performed a half-second dance of derision
Hot stuff flying
Scored to the ribs and boko, tapping the claret
Failed to land a punch all through, but took a dray load
Hooked beautifully on the brisket
Looked like a man who had a toad on toast
The primitive savage, the barbarian
A left to the side neck
Screamingly funny
His once gorgeous bathing gown now a bit faded

6.

So, my uncle said, we learn from this assemblage of fragments firstly that Grim inspired prose purveyors to new levels of purpleness, and we learn that everything he did and everything that was done to him inside the Australian ring had already happened elsewhere. I stayed awake last night rifling the files for a small sample of U.S. news stories in the years prior to Grim's arrival in Sydney. They provide clear evidence of artistic continuum. Now, points you will note in the extracts that follow: the journalistic astonishment, the casual racism, the bewilderment of opponents, the catalogue of damage, and the seemingly universal delight in witnessing a genuine freak. I've underlined the key passages. Here you go:

Delaware County Daily Times, Pennsylvania, 1 December 1902
The comedy bout was the six-round go between Joe Grim, the Philadelphia Italian, and Lon Beckwith the colored middle-weight of this city. Both are big and strong fellows and they went through a hard pace. Grim is one of Lew Bailey's wonders and he is a wonder. He is one of the kind that eats them alive and he had Beckwith very much puzzled. Grim had a funny way of jumping four feet in the air and when he came down to earth again he would land a back-handed blow and get away from Beckwith before he knew what had become of him.

When the big fellows run together in a clinch the sound resembled that made by two freight cars coming in contact and during the hugging match Grim pounded his opponent hard on the kidneys. Referee Lew Bailey had a hard time to get them to break away, and while Grim was doing most of the fighting, Beckwith was doing most of the laughing. When Joe stung him with a hard right that nearly floored him the colored man began to look serious and tried to finish the Italian, but the onrushes of the big Dago were so swift and vigorous that Beckwith was almost finished himself.

In the sixth round Beckwith pulled himself together and went after the Italian better than in any of the previous rounds. He had the big fellow so worked up that he commenced to talk and when Joe talks he is mad all over. He told the audience that he would wager $500 that Jack O'Brien could not put him out. Joe has faced O'Brien and George Cole and both have found him a hard nut to crack. Beckwith said after the go that he is the funniest fighter he has ever faced and the only way to get at him is by using a baseball bat.

Oshkosh Daily Northwestern, 16 October 1903
The fight started with all the elements of a comedy. For three rounds the horse play went on. Then suddenly Fitzsimmons found out that knocking out Joe Grim was no joke. The three last rounds showed a melee of savage punches. In the whirl of the ring could be seen the corrugated brow of Fitzsimmons drawn into a scowl of determination and rage. The pale set face of the Italian, streaming blood and two bodies flecked and spattered with the crimson fluid.

Grim, battered almost to a standstill, hung on in a manner worthy of his name. He showed all the courage of a bull dog, never offering to save himself by clinching.

Chicago Daily Tribune, 18 October 1903
[Bob Fitzsimmons said:] 'I considered it a huge joke when that Italian faced me, so played with him during the first three rounds. I did not let go at him hard, fearing I would bung up my hands. After the third round I tried my best to knock him out and just couldn't. I knocked him down as fast as he could get up, but could not keep him down long enough to have the referee count over him. Tough? Well, I should say. He took enough beating to stop a half dozen men but he wouldn't stay down. Instead he came up smiling, looking for more.'

The Indianapolis Star, 26 October 1903

Told in his own words, his story is as follows:

I am Joe Grim.

That is enough for any man to know.

Who has knocked Joe Grim out? Nobody. It is impossible. Why? I will tell you.

First, I have no fear.

Second, I feel no pain. A blow is something to laugh at. When I am hit on the jaw I shake my head. I think of my ancestors in Naples and the thing is forgotten.

When I got a blow in the solar plexus, where Fitzsimmons hit me five times, I am jarred. For one second it is unpleasant. I gasp. I feel disturbed, but I recover instantly.

When I get a blow on the heart – and I have had many of them put there by big men – I have a touch of regret that the heart is so weak as to feel badly. If my father could see his son he would say: 'Joe Grim is a Roman.'

It is a very hard thing to explain my courage. If I am knocked down it is because I am too light to stand up.

Anybody can learn to box. But to fight it is different.

I am Joe Grim. Nobody can knock me out.

The Houston Post, 1 November 1903

There is a story about Joe Grim that illustrates the toughness of his body. A few weeks ago, while Grim was training, a visitor at his quarters said that Bob Fitzsimmons' solar plexus punch would soon 'do up' the Italian. Grim went away, and in a few minutes returned with a heavy pickaxe handle. He passed it to the visitor, then, holding his arms above his head, invited the scoffing stranger to swing the club and hit him across the stomach. The stranger complied with a will. Grim was knocked to the floor but got up laughing. 'That doesn't hurt,' he said.

I have seen Fitz beat Sharkey to a pulp, double Ruhlin up so that his forehead hit his toes, sink his fist into Corbett's ribs like a soft-nosed bullet into a cheese, batter Jeffries into almost a standstill. Then I saw him use on Joe Grim, deliberately and in deadly earnest, every blow he was master of: and Joe when it was over laughed and turned a somersault.

The Evening World, New York, 23 January 1904
The champion (Joe Gans) had made an agreement to forfeit $100 for every round over six that Grim could stand up and fight.

For marvellous recuperative powers, insensibility to pain and physical hardihood Grim tops anything ever seen in this neck of the woods. Gans fought him furiously the entire distance and dealt out the best blows at his command. And they landed, too. They cut up Grim's lips, made his nose bleed and cut open his left eye until the blood flowed in a stream.

Gans hooked his famous left to the jaw, chopped his right to the jugular, smashed to the wind and sent blows crashing over Grim's kidneys, but all to no purpose.

The Scranton Republican, 22 January 1905
[Reported that after fighting Fitzsimmons, Grim said this from the ring:] 'Ladies an' gentlemens excusa ma I forgotta dat nona de ladies was present, I didda ma besta t-night an I lika a gratta man do Bob fit wacha ma calla him da Gratt Cornish. He no hurta me he try to ana I staya da sixa rouns I lika Philadelph ana I fighta ana da level causa I laka da biz ana I wantta be a da champ. I fighta enny boda no bigga for da Joe Grim datsa da name anna I challenga da bigga himma da Jeff cause ah thinka I like da champ. See Jacka O'Briena, Joea da Walcott, Joe da Gans anna alla da bigga da champ noa bata da Joe Grim because Joe Grim gotta da irona jaw like de bigga hammer anna I like da fighta da Jimma da Corbett anna alla da bigga man. Ima mucha a bliged for a de grata mucha "plause ana godda nighta."'

The Minneapolis Journal, 27 May 1906
Sailor Burke – whose racial liking for the guineas is not marked – sailed into Mr. Grim in a mystifying style. He played a long roll on the face and a 6–8 march on the chest of the Italian who only stuck out his chin to let Burke ruin his hands on the whisker plantation.

Oakland Tribune, 8 May 1908
'Biga de poonch
Biga de mus.
I win biga de fight
From biga de Kaufman.
UGH!'

That was the way that Joe Grim, the iron man of the ring, sized up his chances with Al Kaufman when asked by a *Tribune* representative yesterday what he thought his chances were with the Terrible Blacksmith when they hook up at the Reliance Club next Tuesday night.

That 'UGH!' emitted by Grim was a pip. When Joe was clearing his system of the UGH stuff he spread out his chest like a peacock unwinding his tail. We are not hepped to what UGH means, but we suppose it means no good for Mr. Kaufman.

Of all the rich cards of the ring pugilistic, this boy Grim has the lead by seven furlongs. The fellow is invulnerable to punishment as the hull of a rattling good battleship. The harder he is hit the better he likes it.

7.

I see what you mean, I said. His shtick was well seasoned.

Interesting what humans will pay for, my uncle said. What we actually like. When James Corbett went to England they wanted to entertain him and their idea was to take him to a rat pit and have a champion bulldog kill a thousand rats in a thousand seconds.[6]

I might be interested to see that.

We all would, admit it or not. When you saw Grim in the ring you thought about him and his experience, but what about the shadow side: the other man in the transaction? What must it have been like to strike at Grim with all of your force, to see a man disarmed in terms of any conventional boxing defence, and yet be unable to stop him standing in front of you? Sinking your fist up to the wrist into his midriff, clattering blows off his skull until your knuckles snapped – but he would not be denied. His receptiveness, his pliant passivity, defeated men who possessed the most awesome arsenal of boxing weaponry. It is an inversion without an obvious parallel. The furthest end of a bell curve is something infinitesimal that narrows even further to something barely measurable with a micrometer, and then it narrows further, and then there is a singularity,[7] and then nothing. Grim stands all

---

6   William A. Brady, *The Fighting Man*

7   I once spoke to the UFC heavyweight champion and suggested that if every person on the planet – seven-point-five billion and rising – engaged in a fight to the finish, he would presumably be the winner. He was the last dot on the global bell curve. (Perhaps I was thinking of this famous Muhammad Ali quote, which I have never really understood: 'When you can whip any man in the world, you never know peace.') I asked the world champion if that made his head swim. He wasn't interested. I thought then, and think now, that he was frightened of the isolation. Seven-point-five billion people behind him, and in front of him – what?

on his own at the very extreme of a continuum demarcating individual ability to absorb pain and punishment in a socially regulated context: something 'real' as distinct from the staged vignettes of pro wrestling.[8] The hump of this bell curve descends steeply until there is this, an almost flat line, barely descending, every person represented here extraordinary in their ability to soak up physical abuse, to live

---

8   When I was a lot younger I wrote a catalogue essay for a wrestling-themed art exhibition at a contemporary gallery. Mercifully I no longer have much writing of mine from that time, but this essay survives.* I am interested that its theme was pain, and also interested how mediocre the piece is. I remember trying hard with it; it just came out dead. The catalogue essay was called 'Welcome to the House of Pain'; the exhibition was called *No Holds Barred*. It actually starts okay: 'When you're born they slap you to make you cry, and thereafter pain is one of the few existential certainties. It's a measurement, a currency, an excuse, a motivation.' I don't mind the concluding two sentences either: 'Sometimes pain is a price. Sometimes it's a reward.' The only other bit of the essay to which I'll give a pass mark is about Abdullah the Butcher, not because the words are working so well but just because it was about Abdullah the Butcher: 'As an audience we expect victory to be earned. In the never-square ring the victor has to bear excessive, even outlandish, punishment before his hand is worthy of being raised. Which is not to say that wrestlers have to be sanguine; the only requirement is that they endure their pain, and grace is not a wrestling virtue. I can remember the screaming of a commentator as Abdullah the Butcher was in the throes of agony: 'Abdullah's screaming like a pig, squealing like a pig, as if the dogs have hold of his ears; he's screaming and yelling just as a pig would.' The Butcher, of course, won the bout. If Joe Grim had been born one hundred years later he would have been a professional wrestler.
     Think of the wrestling luminaries famous for being able to take the stiffest bumps – Mick Foley, Sabu, Sick Nick Mondo, Terry Funk, Yukon Eric, who had his ear torn off by Killer Kowalski in Montreal – and then meditate on Grim's capacity as a punishment glutton and his audience-awareness and what a draw card that would have made him.
     * 'A work that's finished is at least finished. It may be poor, but it exists, like the miserable plant in the lone flowerpot of my neighbour who's crippled.' Fernando Pessoa, *The Book of Disquiet*

in that red hell, the line dwindling to dots, until there is a gap, and then, finally, Grim. And then nothingness. How do you make sense of yourself when your next-door neighbour is the void?

He refilled the cracked teacup with sherry and took another slurp, looking pleased with himself.

I spent the night pondering, he said. I started by thinking of Grim in economic terms, a carnival act that made money because he was parlaying a resource of great scarcity. Then I came across something I had scratched together at some point, a fragment of foolscap from down near the door:

> All Grim had to do to make a moderate living was be beaten most-ways to death on a semi-frequent basis. In this, he made public and performative the regimen endured by the boxing sparring partner, a figure with no close equivalent in any other sport. Leading fighters pay lesser fighters to attend their training camps as sparring partners. They work out together most days in a commercial interaction where the lesser fighter is paid a regular wage to take a regular beating. These are rarely men of no talent. Some – Ali's training partner Larry Holmes, for example; José Luis Castillo, who worked for Julio César Chávez; Aaron Pryor, who was sparring partner for Sugar Ray Leonard – eventually make it to the top themselves. But most don't, and stay in the shadow world of trading pain for profit. [9]

---

9   Some might be dealing in odder currency, perhaps: gritty transactions of the soul. Many years ago I watched the workout of a behemoth who would one day become Australian champion (and a world heavyweight champion, albeit for a lightly regarded organization). In a dank suburban gym he was smacking methodically into a grunting, grimacing sparring partner, swinging wide-armed lefts and rights into the man's ribs, snapping his head back with hard jabs, battering him from one corner of the crude ring to the other. The sparring partner was lathered with sweat, his body puffy, and it took me a while to recognize him. He had once been a celebrated footballer. The former household name now had a body like a

Greyhound trainers know that their mutts chase fake rabbits harder once they have had a live kill. Sparring partners sell their agony, and sometimes their health; trainers and managers and topline boxers are prepared to pay the asking rate because nothing else matches the feeling of smashing your fists into a human who can move and moan and bleed. A live kill. For every Holmes, Castillo, or Pryor, there are a hundred men who have never graduated further than 'opponent' rank. You can punch me in the face and the chest and the sides and the shoulders and the neck for multiple three-minute periods six days a week, and I will draw a living wage, and we will both be satisfied. Soaking in the daily assault like it's a Radox bath, basking in the privilege of some primitive connection to another man, or to one's self, or to the outskirts of a machismo-sodden sport, or something clearly external to oneself, an escape.

Good stuff, I said.

Nah, it's fruity. Maybe not purple, but at least a decent deep mauve. The pertinent thing, though, is that Grim was not a sparring partner. Or not often. Probably because he needed an audience as much as he needed his paycheque.

I think I read last night that he was a sparring partner for both Burns and Johnson before the Fight of the Century? Were you there? The first time a Black man was allowed to compete for the Heavyweight Championship of the World?

---

sack of shit and was submitting to the remorseless assault of his employer. I wondered what sort of penance he might have been serving; what sort of abnegation in self-punishment for what perceived sin. Pride, perhaps, the overinflation engendered by undeserved or unsought public reverence (a psychological bear trap baited for feted footballers of all codes), or simply for allowing his body to slump from gorgeous to grotesque? Not that the future was all glitter for the champ; after winning his 'world title' he became homeless, lived on the streets of Las Vegas, was deported from the U.S.A., and died aged fifty-four.

Almost. Not for the fight, damn it to hell. But just beforehand.
And?

I'll tell you. Finish reading those notes I made, though.

Swig.

Why were you making notes? Was there a bigger thing you
were hoping to write?

Who knows, he said. I suppose I thought they would be useful.
And they are. We're setting the table.

I read:

The fight between Tommy Burns, a diminutive sandy-haired
French Canadian, and a piece of living African-American
sculpture from Texas called Jack Johnson was staged in
Rushcutters Bay, Sydney, on Boxing Day 1908. [10] Some revision-
ists have promoted Johnson as the greatest heavyweight of all
time, or one of the top three, but he was probably not in the top
dozen. He had the physique, and a mean streak, and punching
ability, but his defensive-mindedness, the mediocre quality
of many of the men he beat, and the substantial list of quality
fighters (primarily African-American) he chose not to fight
keep him from the top echelon of the heavyweight hierarchy. [11]
For all that, Johnson became a touchstone. Married three times,
always to white women; imprisoned for an offence under the
Mann Act, properly translated as being found guilty of having

---

10   'Considered as potential elements of a story, historical events are value-
     neutral. Whether they find their place finally in a story that is tragic,
     comic, romantic or ironic … depends upon the historian's decision to
     configure them according to the imperatives of one plot structure or
     mythos rather than another.' Hayden White, *Tropics of Discourse: Essays
     in Cultural Criticism*

11   Think of the most terrifying heavyweight performance of all time, which
     – with apologies to Tyson obsessives – was George Foreman demolishing
     previously undefeated Joe Frazier in Nassau in 1973. It is difficult to imagine
     Johnson lasting a minute in the same ring as that version of Foreman.

sex with a white woman; provoking Ku Klux Klan rampages and lynchings because he dared to conquer the master race's finest representatives in the boxing ring – this was a big life. If Johnson bowed his head to anyone it was his father, a short man whose right leg was rendered useless, atrophied from service with the Colored Infantry in the Civil War; Jack called him 'the most perfect physical specimen' he ever saw. Johnson was the most perfect physical specimen many women ever saw; asked once for the secret to his apparently limitless energy by a reporter who had noticed the succession of female visitors to the champ's hotel room, Johnson responded: 'Eat jellied eels and think distant thoughts.'

Tommy Burns, real name Noah Brusso, stood five-foot-seven and weighed 168½ pounds when he faced the Galveston Giant. He was the smallest heavyweight champion in history, but entered the Johnson fight on a sweep of eight consecutive knockouts of bigger men. And, of course, he was white and thus superior. He had already shown something – moral courage, indifference, a willingness to risk, desire for money? – by fighting other African-Americans, a Native American, and at least one Jew (delicately named Jewey Smith). He was married, briefly, to an African-American woman. He has been passed over by aficionados of boxing history, but his story holds more interest than many. There is evidence that he was, at least on occasion, virulently bigoted, but his decision not to dodge Johnson by employing the 'colour bar' opened the door for non-white fighters in the sport's highest-profile division.

Johnson accepted £5,000 for the Sydney bout while Burns was guaranteed £30,000; the disparity may seem grotesque, but it was remarkable that the champion agreed to the contest at all. The event was so controversial it was safest to stage it on the opposite side of the world from the boxing hot spots of the U.S.A. and Europe. The *New York Times* summarized the feelings of many about the cross-racial contest: 'If the black man wins, thousands and thousands of his ignorant brothers will misinterpret his victory as justifying claims to much more than mere physical equality with their white neighbours.'

Johnson defeated Burns, effortlessly, in fourteen rounds and it seemed preposterous afterwards that the result could ever have been different. In the overblown words of that old racist Jack London, who was employed to cover the fight by the *New York Herald*, 'The fight? There was no fight. No Armenian massacre could compare with the hopeless slaughter that took place today. The fight, if fight it could be called, was like that between a pygmy and a colossus … But one thing now remains. Jim Jeffries must emerge from his alfalfa farm and remove the golden smile from Jack Johnson's face. Jeff, it's up to you! The White Man must be rescued.' The old racist Jeffries spouted in turn: 'Burns has sold his pride, the pride of the Caucasian race … The Canadian never will be forgiven by the public for allowing the title of the best physical man in the world to be wrested from his keeping by a member of the African race … I refused time and again to meet Johnson while I was holding the title, even though I knew I could beat him. I would never allow a Negro a chance to fight for the world's championship, and I advise all other champions to follow the same course.' William A. Brady, talking about Jack Johnson in 1916, said, 'A Negro never could hope to be president, governor, or even mayor. But next to that, to be the best fighter in the world, the supreme physical organ of the world, was a great heritage to be handed to a black man.'

Joe Grim was an even more distant outlier than Jack Johnson, but he is never afforded a sinecure in the pugilistic pantheon. His point of difference may have been even more unsettling than Johnson's 'unforgivable blackness'; unlike Johnson he has not been memorialized in more books than a one-legged man could jump over.[12] The supreme hitter is feted in perpetuity. The supreme hittee merely makes things uncomfortable.

---

12   And plays, films, a Ken Burns documentary, a Miles Davis album, songs by Leadbelly and Mos Def, and on and on.

I like that last part in particular, my uncle said, licking his lips.

And you were thereabouts, then?

8.

Almost. I went to watch both Johnson and Burns train in the lead-up to the fight. And last night I located, on the southwest flank of the eastern slope of paper over there, my notes from the jaunt to Sydney.

There was a bookie, a friend of my father's, called Hardheart Harry. He used to come to our place some evenings, never enter the house, just lean on the front doorpost talking low out of the side of his mouth, eyes scanning the street. I don't think he ever spoke two words to me, or me to him. But one night in 1908 he came around, leaned in the doorway, and Dad yelled for me. Said Hardheart wanted a word. Dad had told him how I was mad for the fights. Harry said, It's like this, son. Lotsa interest down here in the Burns-Johnson go-round, and a bloke doesn't want to get burnt. Very bloody hard to get the market right when you don't know the quality of the horseflesh. Reckon I could do with a set of eyes and ears in Sydney town, but the blokes I know up there are all down on me after the spring races. A few of us had the inside word from Johnny Mayo that Lord Nolan was a cert for the Cup, started at sixteens, and the only place we could take full value was interstate. So they're a smidgeon dark on old Harry in the Harbour City. Wonder if you'd like to take a trip up there, snoop around the boxing camps, give me a report. I'll sling you a pound plus expenses.

Two days later I was on the overnight train north, second class. Change at Albury, wander the endless long platform in the sulphur-yellow lamplight, back into the rattler, and sleep till Goulburn. I packed six rounds of cold mutton sandwiches, *The Mystery of a Hansom Cab,* and a notebook containing Harry's addresses for training camps and my fleapit accommodation. It was the best trip of my life. My report:

Dear Mr. Harry (apologies I do not know your surname sir),

Please find following my official Report From Sydney. At the outset please allow me to thank you most sincerely for this opportunity, I will not forget it Sir, I hope with much alacrity that you are satisfied by my report Sir. Sydney is a long way, and I must say they are different people there. I saw some things overnight that I have not seen before and hope not to see again, an eye-opener indeed, and was not a jot sad to rejoin the south-bound train.

Mr. Harry, the overweening truth I want to covey to you Sir is that Johnson will win the fight at Rushcutters Bay. I know that Burns is the favourite, men in Sydney are quoting 6/4 on for the champion, and Johnson is at 2/1 or even 5/2; I heard tell of some-one offering threes on the Negro; I know also that there is no such thing as a sure thing in this life Sir, but I have never been more certain. To go from Johnson's training camp to Burns's is to become acutely cognizant that the size, power, strength and confidence advantages all reside with the Big Fellow. My advice Sir is that if you can get anything better than Evens for JJ you will do a fine thing for yourself. Additionally I think you are safe to take money on Burns at any odds you wish to offer, feel free to sweeten them if there are Big Fish wanting to lay money with you; I may be proven wrong Sir but I do not believe so.

You do not just have my eyes to rely on. I am very Enthusiastic to tell you that I sourced the very best information available locally, That Is, a sparring partner working with both men! I could not believe my fortune. There is a chap called Joe Grim, you no doubt have heard of him, he fought in Melbourne recently, a Philadelphia fighter with a very quaint reputation. He has fought Johnson in the US of A, and some say he has fought Burns as well – he is Opaque on this question, I did ask him – and he was taking a pound per day to work with the two contenders, but remarkable chap that he is, while I was there he worked at both camps on both days without letting on each to the Other. He had some recollection of me from having Crossed

Paths in Melbourne. After his fight with the South African at the Fitzroy Cyclorama.

First, to the Johnson camp. I found it easy enough, he was staying at 23 Anniversary Street Botany.[13] This is a rough and tumble locale, I saw a number of people in the streets that I would not quickly trust, but I must say the Galveston man's actual accommodations are elegant, the Sir Joseph Banks Hotel is a handsome abode although nothing to compare with Collins Street. He is just a few furlongs from the waterfront, the Sea Air would be excellent and there is a sward of park, he can undertake all of his Exercises outside and small wonder his wind is so good. He runs many miles every day, splashes around in the shallows of the bay, good for Healing and Skin In General. He does not have a ring Per Se to work in but there are so many onlookers that they form a perimeter like the old time lumberjack matches. He worked with three different men, all Attired identically in black vests and strides. A fast man and a small man and then lastly with Grim. Grim As You Probably Know offers very little offence, Although, he has been known to wing a big hook occasionally and he tries with his uppercut, but Johnson As You Know is a back-foot fighter; he waits with his enormous length to maximize Time and Space so he can see when the other man is throwing a punch, and either lets it fall far short or else clinches. A bear hug with Johnson; the thought makes me feel odd. He is the most extraordinary Man I have ever seen. The muscles in his back and shoulders, in his neck, the taper at the waist, the Over Developed quadriceps, he may not be a David in the sense of proportions that are Perfection, but he is more machine than man, and I found him simultaneously terrible and, I don't know Sir, unbuttoning. His skin is nothing like our own blacks, it is a different colour and perhaps a different texture, it is satin. There was a mindless piglet mooching about

---

13   There is a seventy-eight-second sliver of documentary film of Johnson's camp, accessible online.

and Johnson insisted on feeding it milk from a bucket, he loved that piglet. [14] Did I Say the Hotel is collocated with a private zoo? It is; built fifty years ago they say. As he came back from his run Johnson spotted a wallaby in a round enclosure. What is that he said. They said a wallaby, native of this Country. Johnson entered the enclosure and chased the wallaby. At first it seemed he wanted to catch the marsupial and then it seemed he wanted to just chase it, and he ran around and around after that wallaby until Finally the wallaby collapsed, I do not know if it expired from the fear and exertion or just Lay Down for dizziness, but Johnson showed his terrible glistening teeth and thought it fine japery. I watched Johnson with all of the sparring partners, the fastest man he saw every punch clearly and reacted with ease, the small man attempted to burrow under but Johnson held him off, arm's length, or threw him backwards, or hugged him into that deep black chest, and every time the Assailant was neutralized Johnson boomed Ho Ho, he enjoyed stymying him very much. And Grim, Sir, Grim he just whaled upon. He pounded out black rhythms, on Torso and Flank and every side of the head. Grim would sometimes be knocked to his knees or even flat on his rump but each time he would resume position, front and centre of the Marauder, and let him pound on him again. Johnson did not enjoy this work so much, he did not boom Ho Ho, he cursed Grim and Grim was the one to laugh, not Ho Ho, but prolonged chortles, and he said you know you will never stop me with your punches tarbaby.

Mister Tommy Burns is living and training in Medlow Bath. He lives in a cottage called Shila owned by Mark Foy, half a mile from the novel edifice of the Hydro Majestic again a wondrous sort of building Albeit the architecture is a Hodge-Podge of taste and styles and really quite unintentionally humorous. Mister Tommy Burns runs all around the hills and valleys, it is very good air and Once Again I think his wind will be excellent, he

---

14   There is newsreel footage of this also.

also Rows on the Artificial Lake, makes use of the handball court Etcetera. He looks to be working hard, he has a ring and an excellent indoors set up. He has an array of sparring partners, and all men are partaking of the wholesome wares at the Hydro Majestic and look well fed. Mister Tommy Burns is a shock in person because he is a Shetland Pony if Johnson is a thoroughbred. I found myself looking downwards toward the top of the head of the heavyweight champion of the world, I did not Truly understand how much shorter than Johnson he is until I stood near, he has knocked cold some of the leviathans of the fistic world, the man must have courage of a puma and a dead punch. He looked very fit but very tight, he Mutters to himself. He works with his men but none of the Partners can replicate Johnson; none is as big, none is as strong, none was counterfeiting his Infuriating techniques for clinching and holding off, smothering and avoiding, only showing interest in striking when all danger of receipt has passed. Mister Tommy Burns spent a lot of time on his footwork, trying to dart out and in, pivoting, changing directions, cutting off space, sliding out of corners. He also is working with Grim, hello Joe he said, always a pleasure My Friend, and Joe said I should have brung you oysters and bananas, no oysters and bananas growing up here, and Mister Tommy Burns laughed good-naturedly. Grim tried to get Mister Tommy Burns to agree to fight him if he kept his World Strap against Johnson but he just laughed and then when Grim kept pressing the Issue he said 'We will see' but did not seem to have his Heart in it. He went to work on Grim then, slashing to the body, working up to the head, graduating back to the soft stomach then northwards through the slats, the neck, the jaw and the temple. Very Nice encouraged Grim who went down three or four times, each time India Rubber and back in position. It was Brusque and Convincing work, and the man who has knocked cold eight straight heavyweights Should, you might think, be favoured. But I was stunned to imagine the two combatants together, to think of what Johnson can do to nullify, and the lack of opportunities Mister Tommy Burns will have to close distance, and thought of Johnson's punches, Murderous when he chooses to use them. And I left Medlow Bath very certain and hence a little sad.

I was afforded a ride in the same carriage as Grim back to the lurid avenues of Sydney and we chatted Some. We were with the correspondent of the *National Advocate* who asked if you were a Betting Man who would you favour and Grim said he would much rather see a white man win any day, but is at the same time of the opinion that Johnson will make Burns bite the dust. [15] I wanted to ask Grim a lot but I confess Sir I was Shy. I did say to him, down the mountain and speeding through the hinterland suburbs, Which man hits hardest? He said it was a question without rationality; that no man on earth could stop Joe Grim. I said I understood this, but was one a harder puncher? He said it was of no accord, if no punch of any velocity could stop him. I said, but what of when they meet? He said, oh, Johnson will Win in a Canter. Burns will not get near him, and the Giant hits like a mule kicks. I wanted to say, Your Body is like a Laboratory, it is amazing, you are a Scientific Instrument for measuring pain. But I did not. Leastways, Sir, I felt that I then had Verification for you from the best possible judge of what my own eyes had learned, and sufficient evidence to provide you with Inside Knowledge. Grim stared out the window or peered into an old leather pouch, and I saw him thumbing pound notes in there and nodding to himself.

This finalizes my report Sir I am again ever so grateful for the opportunity, No Doubt you will have many men wishing to punt on the outcome of the world title fight But I truly believe a dark man will win the Belt for the first time, Johnson is an awesome proposition and I think two Burns could not beat him. I note that all of my transport and lodgings were paid for so there are no further expenses and I look forward to receiving my

---

15   *National Advocate*, 6 October 1908

Pound which you kindly offered, and for you to Clean Up on the Boxing Day contest.

I remain, gratefully and respectfully, your humble envoy and correspondent.

That's pretty great stuff, I said.

Isn't it, Uncle Michael said. You know what else is great? McWilliam's Royal Reserve Sherry. You better duck out and purloin some more.

9.

You make a reasonable point, I said to my uncle: why write a book about pain when there are many sunny aspects of the human condition that could be written about instead? [16] So many other grains of sand. Perhaps because there are ghosts in my head, old horrors and insecurities that link to tropes of masculine behaviour and rural Australia, or versions of same, that existed a long time ago when I was growing up, and that I may have misread at the time, and my mis/apprehensions have metastasized since. [17] Knowing what I know now, it seems certain that on and off from age thirteen I was sick, to a greater or lesser extent, so that swirling obsession with pain, and men, and Australia, and courage, and cowardice, was happening in a mind subject to deep dis-ease. My observations were sharp, but that did not prevent my conclusions going skewiff.

I once saw an artwork that took a slightly imperfect square as its starting shape, my uncle said. The artist then drew around that shape, then again around that, and on and on, until the figures ultimately being drawn were wildly warped. Nothing even approximating a square.

Yeah, that's it. The way my thinking functioned at that time, a slightly incorrect premise or a misguided assumption would become the foundation on which I would construct elaborate ontologies that were spectacularly wrongheaded, and often fervently held.

---

16 'All writing is garbage. People who come out of nowhere to try to put into words any part of what goes on in their minds are pigs.' Antonin Artaud (the cheery scamp), *The Nerve Meter*

17 'We are all serving a life sentence in the dungeon of the self.' Cyril Connolly, *The Unquiet Grave*

My uncle nodded. If you take up residence in your own head for long enough, you start to think you're able to evict the landlord.

Okay, I said. And there was no release. I taught myself not to cry. Not sure how. I didn't cry through my teenage years, and for many years thereafter. Becoming someone who did not and in fact could not cry seemed like an excellent thing. [18] Poor ridiculous fool that I was.

You were trying to build a self that could resist the travails life imposes. It's not unusual. Not heroic, but not to be scorned, either.

If the world existed to inflict pain on me, I would make myself seem impervious, even if I was not. And there was religious stuff brewing around as well, the ultimate goal to become heroic in and through God, hopelessly corrupted by my nascent messiah complex. I lived in an isolated town and I did not meet many people. I did not have the opportunity to read outside the boundaries of the local library and the daily paper. No TV for most of my upbringing, no telephone, no internet, no transport link to the rest of the world. It was easy to imagine I was someone much less than I was. It was also easy to imagine I was someone much more; I remember a period when my fervent praying slid into getting on good terms with the Lord on the sure assumption that at some point I would take my rightful place as a fourth member of the trinity.

That's always good.

Yet at the same time I was preoccupied with every banal thing I saw in front of me. Boys with guns and motorbikes and a fetish for hurting each other. Suicides and road deaths and bullets gone astray and decapitation. Casual cruelty. Dark stories of gang sex and uncertain consent. And me, always watching, always longing to know more, shut away with my Bible and my novels and my off-kilter dreams.

---

18   'Too much of strong/and never enough of vulnerable;/Self-erasure for the comfortable/consumption of others.' Mik Frawley, *For Tyrone Unsworth*

We are an odd breed.

Memories[19] and spectres and grasping toward slippery truth.

Trains on opposite tracks, passing in fog, pathetic whistles howling.

---

19 'What we don't talk about, though, is the wounds inflicted when we write about our wounds.' Emma Goldberg, 'We Need to Talk About the Aches and Pains of Nonfiction,' *Los Angeles Review of Books*

10.

And did you ever see Grim again?

Did I see him again! Yes, I saw him again, my uncle said. Look, it was a long time ago.

It was 1908.

And 1909.

And 1909. When did you see Grim next?

How do I know? I am old. It will be written down somewhere here, but do you want the job of finding my diaries, or my letters, or my notes, or newspaper reports in banks west and east? All of this paper leaves me abject. Defeated. Why did I devote a life to the accumulation of words? Why didn't I commit myself to debauched sex or limitless laughter or feeding stray dogs? Something useful?

I don't have an answer for that, I said, limply. And you seem to be able to find things all right in the word piles. Did Grim stay on in Sydney?

No, his next two fights were in Zeehan and Ballarat. The silver and gold tour. I don't think I was there for the Ballarat stoush, but I might have been. I certainly followed him down to Zeehan in Tassie.[20] It had about ten thousand people at that time. The main street was pub after pub, tough miners tumbling out of every door, and then finally you came to the Gaiety Theatre. A grand sight, sprung floors for dancing, high ceilings, very high tone. I was standing outside the Gaiety on the afternoon of the fight trying to sort out where the tickets were sold, when I felt a heavy hand on my shoulder. I spun around, and it was Grim. I recognize your face, he said. He remembered me from the Cyclorama and also the Sydney

---

20 'What happens might be good or bad, but its happening will be good. Spirit of the picaresque, that.' Alan Gould, *The Poets' Stairwell*

training camps. He already had his cornermen – Charlie Murphy, Bonner, and Daymon. But he said I could be an unofficial fourth. So it was that I sat backstage in the dressing room surrounded by pantomime paraphernalia with Grim and his men as we waited for him to be called to the ring.

Grim was so calm he looked almost glum. Daymon was edgy. Hey, kid, go and find out where the bastards are up to in the program. I sped from the wings to get a look at what was happening in the ring, then darted backstage intermittently to keep them apprised. First up, members of the Zeehan Gymnastics Club gave an exhibition on the horizontal bars, followed by a club-swinging exhibition by a local strongman called Welling. There was a four-round stoush between two sluggers called Goram and Grubb, and a strange two-round show between two local lads with a grudge, Goldsmith and Lynch, with Goldsmith trousering the wagered money. And then it was Grim's turn. When the referee ducked his head into our room and told us to be in centre ring within five minutes, Grim gave a guttural sigh. Then and only then he stood up, went through some perfunctory stretches, and slipped his mitts into the six-ounce gloves provided by the venue. Murphy dragged Grim's trousers off, revealing the trademark pink-and-blue trunks, then draped a gaudy gown around his slumped shoulders. And then the door opened, and it was like flicking a switch and getting electric light. Joe ran out of the dressing room door and whooped loudly all the way to the centre of the arena. A creature transformed. [21]

---

21 'Roman sports derived more from the Etruscans than from the Greeks. Under the Romans sport became a show, a dramatic staged event for the purpose of diversion. The Latin word "ludi" was distinctly Roman. Whereas the Greek word for athletics, "agon," meant a contest, "ludi" was a game in the sense of an amusement or entertainment. The same root word was used for players and actors in the theatre: "ludiones." It was a far cry from the Greek athletic ideal.' William Joseph Baker, *Sports in the Western World*

The fight, as I recall it, was close. It was trumpeted as being for the Heavyweight Championship of Tasmania, and Malley Jackson was a true heavyweight, towering over Grim. But he was not much good. He had lost five on the trot, and only had one victory to his name. Three of the losses were disqualifications, one he quit midway through, and the other came when he was knocked cold in a battle of miners at a shed in Broken Hill. Malley and Joe slapped at each other for twenty rounds, and the Zeehan crowd was peeved when the local man had his arm lifted as the victor.

Grim supplied most of the energy on the night, and seemed offended that Jackson did not provide more interesting competition. 'Grim rushed Malley and ripped in a few body hits. Malley went over a little as if hurt, in the region of the stomach. Joe made another speech. "Good enough for you! You have to stand up to fight me, you know."' [22] When the fight was done we helped Grim back to the dressing room, drained of energy, frowning, preoccupied with getting his money, seeming obscurely disappointed by the event but not, probably, the result. You can run along now, kid, Daymon said to me. I left, reluctantly, and did not see Grim for several months. Everything felt painted with sadness. I can't say why.

---

22   *Zeehan & Dundas Herald*, 5 April 1909

11.

Have I told you about the goat?

You haven't. Who was the goat?

My uncle tipped the teacup upside down to empty every remaining droplet into his mouth, then refilled it. Looked at me. You want to hear about the goat? I can only tell it like it happened.[23]

Like you remember it happened.

Like it happened. I was there, remember.

I shrugged.

So, this is what he told me:

You'd better not fucken eat me, said the goat, straining at the rope that was biting into his neck.

That's lovely language for a goat.

Lovely language for anyone.

We're all in this together, the goat said. If I'm fucked, you're fucked as well.

Lovely sentiment for a goat, Grim said.

Lovely sentiment for anyone, I said.

I enjoy his implication that we might, by any stretch of credulity or possibility, not be completely and comprehensively fucked already, Grim said.[24]

---

23 Maggie Nelson in *The Argonauts* exposes fiction that 'purports to provide occasions for thinking through complex issues, but really it has predetermined the positions, stuffed a narrative full of false choices, and hooked you on them, rendering you less able to see out, to *get* out.'

24 Yes, Grim sounds like a tweedy don here, but he also sounds like the narrator's uncle, who may not be his uncle. I don't care to mimic contemporary newspaper reports' offensive pidgin of 'I fighta enny boda no bigga for da Joe Grim datsa da name anna I challenga da bigga himma'

The goat is generous like that, I said.

Grim had an orange rock the size and shape of Yorick's skull in his left hand. He transferred it to his right. Looked at it, rolled it over, passed it back to his left hand. Then back to his right.

The goat gurned and tossed its head viciously sideways, making the rope cinch deeper into the bristled neck flesh.

Grim looked a little longer at his orange rock, then heaved it away, an arc inscribed against the flat blue sky, a clatter somewhere as it landed. This isn't getting us any closer to Perth, he said.

I thought it would work. I said I'm sorry.

Riding a goat across the continent. Two men, one goat. Even the Masons would balk at that ratio.

You're gonna blame the fucken goat, right, the goat said, words strangled as they emerged. You rode a talking goat to the centre of

---

and we need dialogue to give some interiority to a man who, in life, won attention very largely through deeds rather than words, and if he speaks a lot like my uncle, that is just because this is the way Uncle Michael remembered it. Of course.

'For all historians, however apparently abundant their sources and discreetly narrow their focus, there is a daunting space between those sources and the past worlds which gave them being, but for those of us whose subjects have left few or no words of their own, and whose behaviour we can glimpse only fleetingly through the eyes of outsiders, the gap between fragmented and partial survivals and the complex past yawns massively. There are devices available to mask the gap, and some have enjoyed wide currency. It is possible to proceed as if the fragments are indeed complete representations of past reality, and by cobbling them together, to populate one's pages with radically simplified characters animated by a primitive psychology … Alternatively, if one is troubled by the implausible thinness of accounts so produced, one can attempt to simulate the complexity of reality by projecting one's own common-sense interpretations to lend flesh to the skeletal record, in the eerie conviction that the people of the past are simply ourselves tricked out in fancy dress. But these stratagems merely deny the gap: they do not help us to bridge it.' Inga Clendinnen, 'Understanding the Heathen at Home: E. P. Thompson and His School,' *Historical Studies* the country because there was no other fucken way you could think to get from Melbourne to Perth. You realize the Southern Ocean has been invented?

I hate it when you couch these little barbs as questions, I said, jerking on the rope until a rivulet of blood ran down the goat's neck. Do you know that, eh? Are you aware of this irritating inclination you 'fucken' have?

The goat's eyes bulged white and blue like hard-boiled emu eggs.

All right, sorry I mentioned it, said Grim. Never wanted to be the catalyst for unpleasantness. How are we going to pass the shining hour?

The goat tried to respond, lower jaw spasming, but no sound coming forth. Grim sighed and put his hands inside the noose, loosening it.

I said don't kill the fucken goat, the goat said.

We'll do what we want, I said, sour.

Did I ever tell you – Grim, trying to move our minds somewhere else, keep peace – about the time I was travelling through the country and I saw a farmer in an apple orchard? He had a mob of pigs around him, and one of them was in a big canvas sling, and the farmer had tossed a rope over a branch and was hoisting the pig up into the branches, and the pig was eating apples right off the tree. The farmer looked like he was going into cardiac arrest, sweating and moaning, and I said to him – Old chap, why don't you just wait for the apples to fall off the tree and then the pigs can eat them off the ground? He looks me in the eye and says, Yeah, I guess you could do it that way. I said to him, You know, apart from anything else it'd save a huge amount of time. He thought awhile and said, Yeah, I guess. But what's time to a pig?

The goat brayed and clapped its forehooves on the ground. Very fucken good, it said. The goat was obviously trying to wedge itself into the leaves of Grim's good books.

That reminds me of something, too, said the goat, warming to it, sounding very smug about having a voice again and the power of unrestricted breathing. I walked behind the goat and gave the rope a tug and made the goat yelp, but Grim looked injured and loosened the knot again. As I said, said the goat, it puts me in mind of a time I walked into a farmhouse with a farmer. We went into his bedroom and there's the farmer's missus in bed. The farmer says, This is the pig I have sex with when you're not interested. She looks at us, nasty like, and says, I think you'll find that's a goat. The farmer says, Yeah, and I think you'll find it was the goat that I was talking to.

Good, said Grim. Venerable, and alarmingly sexist, but very good.

Well, I said. Pigs. Let's stay with pigs; keep away from ignorant creatures like goats. I'm out in the bush once and I come to this farm and there's the farmer and he's got a pig there nuzzling up against him, rubbing his whiskers into his trouser leg, and the farmer every now and then bends down and kisses the pig on the head, and the pig smiles; it's hard to believe a pig can smile, but this one smiles like a fat happy baby. This pig is such a cute thing, but it has a wooden leg. I ask the famer why the pig has a wooden leg and he says, Well, a while back now I was plowing the back paddock and the tractor tipped over and the pig saw what happened, came over, and pushed the tractor off me enough that I could escape. Wow, I said, and it damaged its leg doing that? No, no. There was another time I was in the top paddock and a tiger snake comes up behind me, about to strike. The pig sees it and comes over and tackles the Joe Blake and saves my life. Did the snake bite its front leg, I ask. No, no. Come to think of it, there was also the time when the farmhouse caught on fire and the pig raced in and woke us all up, saved me and the wife and the kids. I say, The leg was burned then, was it? No, not at all, the farmer says. Well, I just don't get it, I shout at the bloke, why the dickens has it got a wooden leg? Oh, that's not difficult to answer, says the farmer. I mean, a good pig like that, you'd never eat it all at once.

Grim laughed, but the goat curled its long top lip. Joke's fucken older than Methuselah, he said.

Yeah, and your joke's got a grey beard and all, I said right back at him.

You two, said Grim, looking vexed. It's not helping. It's not stopping us dying out here a million miles from where we are supposed to be. Not doing my stress levels any favours.

You got any better ideas to get us through the day?

I don't know, he sighed. I guess I could give you my memoirs.[25] A disquisition on the life and times et cetera.

Should I build a fire? Get out the slippers? Hot cocoa? (This did not come out sounding as sarcastic as I had hoped.)

As you please. I was not always the man you see before you. Not always Joe Grim. Not always eloquent and urbane. As you know, Grim is my part, and I'm happy to play it. But all those ughs and oofs and spaghetti-tongued malapropisms, all of the broad-brush caricaturing, it's grotesque pantomime and I tire of it frequently. I mean, it's what they want, it's generative of lurid public attention and thus an income. But just because it's a necessity does not mark it a pleasure.

---

25 'In a work of nonfiction we almost never know the truth of what happened … In imaginative literature we are constrained from considering alternative scenarios – there are none. This is the way it *is*. Only in nonfiction does the question of what happened and how people thought and felt remain open.' Janet Malcolm, *The Silent Woman: Sylvia Plath & Ted Hughes* (her italics)

    There are tidbits I excavated in research that could have been used to construct a larger and more nuanced portrait of Grim: that he was charged with robbery (and later acquitted); that he had a terrible gambling habit; that he could be hotheaded. It may be equally likely that the opposite was true; the probability of a self-promoting ethnic outsider being represented with precision and verity in the American press more than a century ago seems slight. But I don't care, because I am interested only in Grim as a pain eater.

Fucken A, said the goat.

I was, as I think you already know, born in Avellino in southern Italy on 16 March 1881. Birth name Saverio Giannone. My family had no money. Never. But I discovered a way to earn some cash. Simplicity itself. The Avellino Cathedral; you possibly don't know it.

Yeah, quite fucken possibly.

Avellino Cathedral – built between 1132 and 1163, updated in the nineteenth century to current neoclassical appearance. It has huge bronze doors displaying scenes from history. Our history, not yours. These enormous doors, towering things, foreboding, flanked on either side by marble statues of Saint William of Vercelli and Saint Modestinus. Then above the doors, in a semicircular lunette, a bas-relief of Christ and his confreres at the Last Supper.

You are a fucken font.

Campania, my region, we invented pizza. Calzone, meaning literally 'trouser leg.' Mozzarella cheese. Perhaps Neapolitan ice cream, I don't know; I don't think I ever went to Naples. Mainly I only remember the hazelnuts. That's what my parents did – collected baskets and bushels and boatloads of hazelnuts. This was not lucrative work. We were not wealthy people.

The goat yawned. Enough etching of fucken detail, bit of fucken narrative movement, thanks.

I was squalidly gratified to see the goat had stopped trying to win Grim's favour.

The only sibling I cared about was my older brother Giordano. He had polio and no use of his legs at all. He used to traverse the streets on his hands, begging for alms, or sometimes dancing on his wrists and elbows for passing travellers. I used to follow him around, and whenever anyone tried to get rough with him, which was about every day, I would intercede and take the beating for him. I loved Gio so deeply. So deeply! One day we saw a man who had both legs amputated, walking the streets of Avellino on his hands like my brother, but he had special leather boots fitted to his palms. Gio was entranced.

Sav, this would make all the difference to me, he said. We went to the local boot maker and he traced out the shape of Gio's hands and showed us the high-grade hide he would use to construct the hand shoes. And then he told us the price. It was more than my parents earned in a month collecting hazelnuts. It was an impossible sum. Gio looked at me and his dark eyes were like black olives and his lips pinched together, and he didn't say anything. What could be said. I asked the boot maker if there was any possible discount, but he said he was a poor man, he had thirteen children all going hungry and the sum he mentioned was cost price. We shuffled out and Gio tried to dance for money in the main street, but his whole body was rinsed with sadness. I tried to dance for him, I tried so hard, but I am not constructed that way, I could not remember which limb to move and in what sequence, and we went home that day without earning even the smallest coin. Gio was slower than ever, a rainstorm had made the cobbled streets slick and ugly, and he toppled several times as his hands slipped in discarded slops and animal ordure.

The coarse pink sand I was using as a daybed had compacted beneath me. I ached. I rolled to my feet, brushed all the sand and pebbles from my person, then, lacking any alternative, slumped down in the trench of sand again as Grim ground on.

Gio seemed to slip into a funk. It continued for days. Weeks. Not only did he stop dancing, but he could not even motivate himself to beg. He would still come out on the streets with me but then just slump there, useless legs splayed across the footpath, irritating the denizens of the town, drawing more opprobrium, leading inevitably to more physical confrontations that I needed to defuse. We would scout the bins for food but otherwise they were purposeless days. I could not dance and he would not play mendicant, and with genuine objects of misery like Gio on the streets it was pointless for an able-bodied nine-year-old like me to try begging. I did, sometimes, but went whole days without so much as a single centesimo. We were chased from place to place by irate shopkeepers, restaurateurs, polizia. One day we were pushed to the patch of public space in front of the cathedral. I harried the churchgoers, to no financial effect.

I feel we are approaching the tipping point of the yarn, said the goat, with the key quandaries about to be refuckensolved, namely: Could you make greater utility of the meagre resources you had? Was there any way to inveigle moolah from the passersby in that gritty city in those difficult days? But a reminder we could do with a modicum more fucken rapidity.

En pointe, Grim nodded to the goat. So yes: we found ourselves talking about the great iron doors of the cathedral. One child claimed that if your head collided with the door it would be left with an indelible imprint from the bas-relief in the metal. It was postulated that someone should verify whether this theory was correct. I volunteered, on the proviso that money was sought from bystanders. [26] I think the total raised was just over two lira, a lot of money for us then, relatively. I insisted that the money had to be given to my brother to hold before I would perform the experiment. This duly took place. I remember feeling equable. The prospect did not worry me. People pushed forward in a horseshoe shape, they counted down from dieci to uno, and I started running as hard as I could. Up the sixteen shallow steps, arms pumping, then a heroic headfirst dive into the meat of the iron door.

There was a roar of acclamation and amazement. People shouting, Is he dead? The noise, they said, reverberated a mile in every direction. I was grabbed by the spectators, who pawed at my skull, trying to find any evidence for or against the theory. Sure enough, embossed across my forehead was a reverse image of Saint Sabinus. More roaring. People talking of my courage, freakishness, et cetera. I offered to do it again. There was less money this time, but still

---

26 Several sources, all of them secondary, tell the story of the child Giannone/ Grim making money by running headfirst into the cathedral door.

more than a lira. If anything, I ran even harder, careened up the sixteen steps, pinned my arms to my sides, and dove with all my might into the door. Headfirst.

Again: acclamation, amazement, roaring. The noise roused a young priest, who emerged snarling through the cathedral's entrance, asking what the carry-on was about, shooing everyone away. Apparently confession was interrupted because parishioners thought an earthquake had seized Avellino. We decamped then, but the next day returned to seek funds from intrigued citizens for a repeat performance. Gio would collect the money and give a little spiel, I would invite the pavement strollers to inspect my skull with their eyes and hands, then I would execute the deed. Headfirst into the giant cathedral doors. Then one of the priests would threaten us with hellfire, which didn't bother us, or the constabulary, which did, and we would disperse until the next day. This became our pattern.

Devilishly fucken clever, said the goat, but what toll did it take on your noggin?

My head was fine, hence the ineluctable conclusion: I had discovered my talent, and thus a vocation. The trauma to my scone was negligible and only ever superficial – the skin split or welted. I realized that people enjoyed the blood, and this was good for earnings, and over time it dawned, also, that I liked the cynosure modality; to wit, I enjoyed the attention. I liked the gasps and also the cheers and even the inevitable interminable coda when patrons would run their hands all over my skull and body. I asked once if they would like to poke a paw into the wound in my side, but, of course, we were and are a Roman Catholic country and the bon mot was not gladly received.

Who was this Sabinus fucker, said the goat. I am not well acquainted with his story, notwithstanding mind you that I've never met a goat that owns his or her own copy of *The Lives of the Saints*.

Not to say, of course, no such goat exists, but that is the truth of my own experience, and that is of fucken all I can speak.

Saint Sabinus was a folk hero and religious icon where we were raised. You will recall – perhaps even you, goat, despite the obvious limitations of your personal library – that Diocletian wanted all Christians put to death around 300 CE, and snaffled their estates into the bargain. Sabinus was preaching the Word so Diocletian tasked governor Venustian with removing him. He had Sabinus's deacons scourged, bashed with clubs, ripped with great iron nails, then torn apart with metal hooks. Sabinus was tossed in jail, then they cut off his hands.

Not fucken great for wiping your arse, said the goat.

Maybe not his most pressing concern, said Grim. Anyway, while he was in jail he cured a young prisoner's blindness. Venustian had poor eyesight himself. He asked to visit Sabinus, and he fixed his vision, too. Optometry by faith. Sabinus converted Venustian to Christianity, a fine effort although it didn't bring his hands back. The Powers That Be did not enjoy this twist in circumstances and had Venustian, his wife, and sons beheaded.

And Sabinus lived happily ever after.

No, they took him to Spoleto and smashed him to death with lumps of wood. [27] This is a big story where I grew up. I used to cogitate on it: Could I have survived the attack at Spoleto? If I was Saint Sabinus I could have withstood that beating, I'm sure of it. Hands or no hands. Lumps of wood or no lumps of wood. There is no physical assault of that nature I cannot endure.

Good for fucken you, said the goat. But that means they would have done you with the nails and the hooks and the scourges. I assume you bleed like other mortals.

---

27 Reminiscent of the story recorded by W. G. Sebald in *After Nature* of the peerless sculptor Riemenschneider, who was condemned to have his hands broken while held in a torture cell by the Würzburg bishop.

So now we know why you're the way you are, I said.

Who can say? Biology is destiny. Cultural heritage is destiny. National identity is destiny. My hard head is destiny.

Enough of the ten-buck words, said the goat. We get the point: you are counterintuitively intelligent, urbane, fucken voluble. But hose down the king shit vocab. I grew up in the country; that sort of verbiage can get you badly hurt. Just shanghai back to the narrative fucken thread and give it to us plain and simple.

I was trying to make a point. Don't assume I'm any more stupid than you. But okay.

Where were we? Oh yeah, seeking coins at the cathedral. Gio and I were able to take home small sums of money most days. I thought we had enough cash to get the hand shoes made, but whenever I asked Gio to show me the tally he would just say, It's growing all the time, don't worry, trust me. That was what he always said, grabbing my arm and looking into my eyes like he could see into the back of my brain: Trust me. But I was working so hard, and I was just a little kid and I needed to see that we were getting somewhere, so one night as he slept I rolled up the corner of the mattress where he tucked the money at the end of each day. There was nothing there.

A fucken junkie, shouted the goat. Or was it a gambling thing?

Neither. I didn't know what to do. I did not want him to know I'd breached his trust, but I was damned if I could continue the performances without knowing we could soon buy the hand shoes. I waited a day, then a week, then a month; each day, off to the cathedral, headfirst into the doors, finishing a bit dazed and covered in red marks but still earning. And then one day, I don't know why, I snapped and asked him where all the money had gone. He did not even look disappointed in me. He said, I wondered when you would ask. I know you looked. Saverio, I said to trust me, and that's all; you have to trust me. I said, But where is the money? And he said, Trust me. Those eyes looking through my eyes again, seeing inside my mind.

And all this time he is still walking on his hands, and the skin is worn to buggery and also that stuff you mentioned about ordure, I said.

The truth[28] was, the sort of money we were earning each day, we should have been able to buy his hand shoes with even one week's takings, two at the most. It was frustrating. So I came up with a plan for a one-off event where we could earn enough in one go to pay the boot maker. There was a man in our town who was the biggest man anyone had ever seen; people said he was the biggest man in Italy, and maybe he was. His name was Jacopo il Gigante, or that is what everyone called him. I went to see him one day and told him what I wanted to do, and he thought about it a lot, and he said he would take part for half of the total earnings, but I begged him – this skinny nine-year-old, standing as high as his kneecap – and the giant was as kind as he was large, as soft as he was strong, and against his better judgment he agreed to assist me for free. I returned to my patch outside the cathedral and started to make my pitch. I yelled as loudly as I could for hours at a time that I, Saverio Giannone, would no longer perform my door head-butt trick. I said it had become too easy. Without meaning. I said that I needed a true challenge, and that Jacopo il Gigante would provide that challenge. I said that on the Saturday two weeks away, as the cathedral clock struck midday, il Gigante would tie my arms to my sides with ropes, then bind my legs together. Once I was made into

---

28 'These various fictional permutations of the past indicate the extent to which there is collective self-conscious awareness of "histories" rather than History. Such variability raises the question as to what desire is being satisfied, or at least momentarily satiated, in the construction of the author's particular choice of narrative?' Timothy Gauthier, *Narrative Desire and Historical Reparations: A. S. Byatt, Ian McEwan, and Salman Rushdie*

a missile unable to move my limbs, Jacopo would carry me to the top step. People could then come forward and stuff money into my pockets. The giant would count the cash as it was deposited, and once there was fifteen lira he would lift me like a log, swing once, twice, thrice, and throw me with all his might headfirst into the mighty iron doors of Avellino Cathedral.

Fuck, said the goat.

Yes. Every day I hollered my news. Noon on the second Saturday! Right here in front of the church! Bring your money, money, money. Would the boy be dashed to death? Could any human survive such trauma, let alone a skinny malnourished child? Who would be responsible for cleaning the metal door of its brains and gore if the giant's strength proved lethal? Who would possibly want to miss such a spectacle? Giordano was extremely agitated; first, because every day that I spent spruiking was a day on which I was not performing and earning money, and second, because he believed I would be killed.

And were you?

You are a moron, said the goat.

Oh yes, I said. But you could have been.

Oh yes. Very much. I loved small parts of my life – remnants of pizza thrown outside café doors, still hot and delicious; the nights when Gio would place his big hand on my head as I settled to sleep; the smell of rain sliding off hot red roofs – but I was not strongly connected to the world. Most of every day was hard. If it was the end of me, this was not the worst outcome.

And, said the goat. What the fuck happened?

What happened. The Saturday was bleak. A black sky squeezing every last goccia of rain onto the streets. Kids in rags trembling with cold. The marketplace unusually quiet. Gio and I arrived to the cathedral early, and there were fewer people about than usual. This was still the case at eleven, and eleven-thirty. But as the big hand on the cathedral clock crept toward the top, a sudden increase. A lot of people, buzzing, stepping from foot to foot, trying to stay warm but also, you know, because of anticipation. This was a great thing. Just before midday, when Jacopo arrived, there was a murmur that turned to a roar. He picked me up and stood at the top of the cathedral steps and shouted for quiet. He said that unless there was fifty lira forthcoming there would be no show. The crowd squabbled and cavilled that the deal had been fifteen lira, but the giant would not budge. Soon there were hands coming forward proffering coins and notes. He counted carefully, or I thought he did, and when twenty lira was collected he reached into his bag and pulled out a length of stout rope. A snarl of excited sound. More hands, more money. Thirty lira. He whirled the rope theatrically, then grabbed me, growling, and lashed my legs together. That seemed to pique the patrons, and more money was produced. Forty lira. He bellowed loudly and unfurled his second piece of cord and tied it round and round my body, pinning my arms to my sides so tight the flesh might have been sewn together.

Damn, I said.

Where is the money, shouted the giant. This child might live or this child might die, and the only way you can find out is by paying for the privilege of discovery. So far he only has twenty lira. Where is the rest? He glared at the assembled throng, outsized eyes bulging, huge yellowed teeth bared, football-sized fists on hips. People in the crowd nudging one another, hassling their fellows to cough up. Jacopo gesturing them forward, double-counting the cash, declaring half the tally, whipping them to a frenzy, until the two pockets of my breeches were groaning with lira. And then, finally, it was time. Jacopo hoisted me, held me parallel to the ground like a battering ram. The crowd started to count: tre, due, uno. Nothing. Again, more raucous: tre, due, uno. Jacopo did not move. The noise even more fevered, an edge to it now, like a wave curling over, moving from enthusiasm to nastiness. The giant bent his huge shaggy head toward me. I can't do it, he muttered. You have to, I said. It will kill you, he said. I can't have that on my shoulders. I can't murder a child. It's not your choice, I said. Without this, I do not have the money. Without the money, Gio has no shoes for his hands. If you fail to throw me with all your effort and might, you betray me, and those people might tear every part from my body because they are so angry, and then I will be dead but for no money.

Tre, due, uno. The monolithic head turning, looking at the crowd. He licked his lips, tongue like a bullock's. He looked back at me. I nodded quickly. Tre, I said. Due. Uno.

Even then a hesitation.

I thought he wasn't

Going to.

But.

A life blur, a smudging, the sense, momentarily, of cold as I was released from the hot hold of those huge hands, and then exhilaration, so fleeting, of flying, and the proprioceptional sense even in that dumb swirling moment to hunch my shoulders around my ears to try to protect my neck, and then the collision, the no awareness in that spatial space of what exactly, what, transpiring, the sense first of incalculable force, of compression, of my feet travelling forward so far that they might come out of my ears, and then the recoil, and about then, then or about that time, the sound began or, more, I started to hear the sound that was already there, a sound like doom, so loud, the metal doors vibrating like the skin of a drum and the whole holy sanctum its reverberant body, this sound such mortal terror, and as I adjusted scandalized to the sound enveloping me, filling all of Avellino, I felt myself bounce as a rubber ball, ricocheting off the great doors and bouncing back to the top of the steps. Powerless to halt my movement, limbs still trussed, head thrumming like a gong from the noise and gaggle, and began, begun, to slip down toward the sea foam froth of bubbling crowd. And then I lost a moment, perhaps two moments, and then I was in the space again, in my body again, and screaming to be loosed from the ropes, because being bound bothers me, and il Gigante was there, blocking the onrush with his great oak bulk, and he slithered me from the strings, and lifted me, folded me tight to his own body, and held me on display for the acclamation of all, and it was mighty.

What damage, I said.

A bit of a fug, my vision was rounded at the edges and my head hurt and my neck ached and I felt like I needed to sleep for a hundred years, but it was really okay. And then I realized why Jacopo had lifted me up, because the eager hands wanted to grapple all over my body, feeling for broken bones, feeling for boards inserted beneath my hairline, perhaps, to make real with their hands what they could barely apprehend with their eyes, but also, crucial this, the giant knew that some of those hands would also worm into my long pockets, and he refused to have me robbed of a single centesimo. In time there was a chorus of cheers, and I sang gaily to the crowd to cheer for Jacopo also, and they did, and gradually the street was swept clear of citizens and we were back with the drizzle and the wind that hit our bodies like ships, except we were rich. Jacopo insisted on accompanying us home in case any thieves were lying in wait for our money, but I insisted that we go first to the home of the little boot maker. When we arrived there, some or all of his children were arrayed across the front step, and they told us that the boot maker had taken ill and was running such a fever that he would not open that day or the next, but to try again on lunedi. We farewelled the giant outside our home, my head still quivering from noise and perhaps also, yes, the violence done to it, more than a little sore now, truth be told, and that day and the next I stayed very close to our premises and refused to remove my clothes, keeping the notes and jiggling coins tight to my body. Not a single lira would go under Gio's mattress, I told him, because he could not be trusted and now we had enough money for three pairs of hand shoes and some new warm clothes for him besides. He didn't argue, but looked in my eyes again, and I looked back into his, like gazing into a gently rippling pond. And when he went to bed I went to bed also and took up my position beside him, nose to nose, and stayed awake as long as I could with my hands clamped hard on my pockets, and then when his breathing changed I blinked into sleep myself. In the middle of the night I woke and thought I heard someone leaving the room, and grabbed for my pockets reflexively, but the cash was untouched. I dreamed of the good-smelling leather on Gio's new hand coverings, and the places we might go together, and how content he would seem inside the thick short coat I would buy him from the royal market, and then the rain could rain all it wanted. And then I woke in the morning, to the good smell of woodsmoke and the muted rumble of post-dawn Sunday, and reached my hand to Gio's body. And he was dead.

The goat gasped, then tried to disguise it as a cough.

I lost him in the night. I wondered if it was the fearful cold of the previous day. I wondered how I did not feel the wings of the black angel flutter as they were wrapped around my beautiful brother's corpse. I stumbled from our mattress and went to alert my parents. On the way, I saw movement in the small glass propped by the washroom door. I realized the movement was me, and looked in the glass for clues, and saw a head that looked like a rotted gourd, blue-black and violet, swollen into uneven lumps, and I shook my head at the shaking head in the glass and rechecked my pockets and went to find my parents. I knew we needed money to bury Gio, and I volunteered the money from my person. My mother and my father watched gravely as I produced coin after coin, note after note, piled high on the pine crate table, and they totalled it as one hundred lira due to the giant's clever double-milking of the crowd, and then they told me that this doubled the sum they already had, the money squirrelled by Gio and given to them for safekeeping to purchase passage away from struggletown Avellino, away from blasted Italy, to the prosperity of the United States of America.

Not gambling or whoring after all, said the goat.

We buried that beautiful brave boy, the one I loved more than any before or since, and with the other money and their proceeds from the hazelnut foraging we had just enough to sail for Philadelphia. I was ten when I arrived on that shore, and never left again until Australia now. All the way on the steamer from Napoli to the U.S.A. I thought about my beloved brother. And it is strange: every nautical mile from Oakland to Sydney, this time, I thought of him again. That is how grief works sometimes: we are reminded by a sight or a sound or a sensation. It is why anniversaries of death are so hard: the trees look the same, the wind comes from the same quarter, the flowers smell a certain way, so the mind is thrown into constant remembrance. I think it was like that on the ship. I would not even say it was unpleasant. It was just something aggressively present, and I had to think of him whether that was what I chose or not, and it hurt but also at one level it was lovely to just hold him there inside my mind and my heart again.

I rolled again out of my desert ditch. I decided to take a short walk. The direction didn't matter; every compass point from here was equally bereft of context. I brushed myself off, nodded to Grim and the goat, and went away for a while, the breeze cooling my cheeks.

12.

My uncle handed me a tattered manila folder that contained the
following information:

Dr. Carleton Simon, [29] noted alienist and criminologist, examined Joe Grim in October 1903. 'Joe Grim, the Italian pugilist,
is able to stand the terrible beatings to which he has lately been
subjected simply owing to the fact that he is in possession of
a very small brain. He is of such a low order of intelligence
that his nerves, which carry the news to his brain when he is
hurt, find a very chilly reception. Now, to grasp the idea that
he has been hurt at all, and then not able to take hold of it with
one-half the sense of pain of a human being of ordinary intelligence, Grim will have to be almost killed before beaten into
insensibility.

---

29 Two years prior to meeting Grim, Dr. Simon was commissioned to make
a psychiatric slash phrenological assessment of Leon Czolgosz, anarchist
assassin of President William McKinley, prior to Czolgosz's execution.
One year after meeting Grim, Dr. Simon was gifted the brain of transport
czar George Francis Train, dissected it and submitted a report to the
American Institute of Phrenology. An MD at nineteen, Simon made
lasting contributions to forensic science and few to psychiatry or
neurocriminology. He loved the spotlight and the bully pulpit, had a
high profile with the New York police force and in Hollywood as a crimes
consultant to the Hays Office. When he wrote about fish and fishing,
which he did extensively, he used pen names that included John O'Neill,
Grape Juice, and Baron Munchausen. In his 'Homosexualists and Sex
Crimes' paper, presented before the International Association of Chiefs
of Police at Duluth in September 1947, he applauded and recommended
the approach taken by the state of Illinois whereby 'homosexualist
psychopathic individuals' were held as involuntary psychiatric prisoners,
then, once they 'recovered,' they could be tried for committing sodomy,
punishable by up to ten years in prison.

'The fact that this man Grim can't grasp the idea that he has been hurt when subjected to physical abuse that an ordinary man could not endure does not necessarily mean that he is not as intelligent as the ordinary human being in other respects. Just as the Human Pin Cushion of the circus side show can stand up and have pins jabbed in his anatomy all day long without feeling any pain, so probably is it with Mr. Grim. He is able to take a heavy blow on the jaw which touches the nerves that take the quickest route to the brain cells, it has no apparent effect upon Grim because his nerves are abnormally sluggish.'

13.

I don't want to lecture you, my uncle said, and then he lectured me
– the act that always follows that locution, which is always irritating.

What is the thing we call pain? It is something that captures the
attention of the sufferer, but otherwise has no meaning. It makes
no sound, has no colour or smell, occupies no physical space. And
yet at its most extreme, pain becomes the only thing of which the
sufferer is aware, bigger for the victim in that instant than any
object in the universe. The nociceptive pathways, which transmit
and receive pain signals and determine how we perceive pain, are
developed prior to birth. You are born, to a greater or lesser extent,
with a pre-existing capacity to feel pain. Jerome Kagan's theories
about high reactivity[30] in infants corresponding to high sensitivity
in adults make intuitive sense.

I have always had metaphorically thin skin, I said, and I have
always observed others who don't, and been perplexed.

What is your pain tolerance?

At different times in my life I have thought that I have a reasonably
high capacity to endure pain, and at other times I have suspected
that I have an unusually low tolerance. Most men (almost all?) like
to think that they have above-average pain tolerance. Research
suggests that people with unipolar (rather than bipolar) depressive
disorders show low pain tolerance, yet paradoxically during periods
of acute depression I have at times felt impervious to physical pain.

Okay, he said, resuming the lecturer role. Contrary to expecta-
tions and popular belief, regular exposure to pain does not necessarily increase pain tolerance. Rather, it can sensitize the victim

---

30 Jerome Kagan, *The Temperamental Thread: How Genes, Culture, Time,
and Luck Make Us Who We Are.*

so that decreased stimulus is subsequently required to produce an equivalent level of perceived pain. This phenomenon seems highly unlikely for a pain artiste such as Grim, or for fighters in general, but maybe this is something they practise concealing, something an onlooker cannot generally know.

In the scientific context (rather than the context of the torture chamber, the schoolyard, the boxing ring), surprisingly few mechanisms have been devised for testing pain tolerance in humans. A lot of knowledge about pain has been derived via experiments on animals. The best-known animal pain experiment is the Randall-Selitto test, where an animal's paw is inflamed (often through the injection of a dry yeast suspension), then pressure is applied to the inflamed area. The animal is regarded as exhibiting a pain response once it starts to struggle. This test is usually enacted on rats and mice. High-profile research has shown that big sea slugs, aplysia, creatures obviously very different from mammals, can demonstrate a learned response to pain.[31]

I said, It may be my thin skin, but I feel like there is something sad about sea slugs locked in laboratories, far from home, fated to be repeatedly tormented in order to have their flinching tested and recorded. Poor bastards. Or perhaps responding sentimentally to the travails of dumb invertebrates is evidence of me being sensitized; the emotional pain I have felt in the past means less potent stimuli are needed to trigger the same response. Some of this sensitizing occurred during the half-year I worked at the back of a very large hospital, right beside the city's leading medical research centre. I have no idea what they were working on in there, and the walls and

31 'After a potentially painful event, there are also examples of modifications in motivation that demonstrate the significance of a damaging event in terms of learning, avoidance and altered behavioural decisions based upon the experience associated with tissue injury.' Lynne U. Sneddon, 'Pain in Aquatic Animals,' *Journal of Experimental Biology*, 2015

windows were thick, but the screaming of the animals in that place was something I cannot forget. I don't know what they were – my guess from the volume and the voice was dogs and monkeys – but their screaming was a distillation of pure pain. And it went on, and on, and on.

14.

I walked for a short eternity, feet sometimes skating on loose gibbers, other times sinking into the pillowy pink sand of dry creek beds. Inscrutable bloodwoods, daubs of dry spinifex, stumpy-tailed geckos and skittish netted dragons, indents of bird feet and snake slither inscribing the earth. A gesture of breeze, just enough to make the desert oaks moan, a mournful unison. When I paused and shuttered my eyes, I could hear, perhaps, each needle of each desert oak breathing its own sound, like the dread realization that you are identifying in isolation individual raindrops on a corrugated iron roof in a night storm. I opened my eyes and the desert oak sound was a long rumbling freight train; I closed them again and each needle was whispering. I was frightened, and then I was tired, and I walked back to Grim and the goat and slumped back into my trench, and wished we had water and that we were not about to die.

And that is why I thank you for your fucken story, droned the goat, the courage and the clarity, the way it shades in the pencilled outline of what I thought I knew, etfuckencetera. As for me, so much to tell, so little time, or so much to tell and so much time, I am not sure. Difficult, really, to select what may be pertinent. There is one thing you might fucken like. However. When I was a younger goat, I was cooped up in a town, a bumfuck hamlet Satan himself would not stop overnight in. The town had special days called drink days, they happened maybe five times a month, where all the yokels would gather outside the only pub and lie in the dirt and drink, start guzzling at sun-up and drink through the middle of the day, drink until they fell asleep in the blazing arvo sun, then fucken wake up and start fucken drinking again, last drinks at midnight, a fucken delight as you can rightly imagine. One day a traveller came to town, a seller of something, I do not fucken remember, perhaps farm insurance or perhaps saucepans, it really matters fucken not. He rode into town on a cheap buggy pulled by a withered horse and it was drink day. It might have been early arvo when he clattered in, we were two hours' ride from the nearest town so he had to stop, like it or fucken not, to spell the horse and get it some water and feed. And being early arvo it meant every man in town was already roaring with it, spread-eagled across the main track through town, fucken splayed across the duckboards outside the pub, slurring and slurping and fucken getting their drink on, because they had not drunk this much since the last drink day, which was fucken five or six days prior. So no wonder they were thirsty and eager to be on it. And the salesman unfolded himself from his fucken buggy and looked like he wanted nothing to do with anything at all but the only way he could get some water and feed was to ask, so he edged to the bloke lying furthest from the pub, dungarees painted grey with road dust, and the cove made his inquiry, very fucken polite like. The drunken bushie didn't answer, just waved his fucken bottle at him and looked away. So the salesman crept along to the next bloke, and he was ignored again. This kept happening, and he made a fucken big fucken mistake and said something out the edge of his mouth about this blinking town and its blankety inhabitants. What's that you said, said one of the bushies, a big one, all four front teeth missing so he could poke the neck of his beer bottle straight into the maw and tip it unimpeded down his throat without opening his jaw and risking letting in flies. The fuck you said? Nothing, said the cove, and that was fucken stupid. What's your problem, said the big fucken bully. Are you a Chinese are you, son? No, said the cove, I'm not Chinese. Well are you a woopsy, cos you look like you're a woopsy. No sir, there's no nance in me. What about a Jew dog banker, mebbe that's your game? No, nothing of the sort, and I was just hoping to be pointed toward a place to water my horse, and maybe a bit of feed. Well are you one of those spider-fucking

Catholics we keep hearing so much about? Well, maybe I am that, said the cove, squirming under his mediocre suit. All the heads spun toward him like they were attached to swivels and not necks. Bottles were put down, there was a what-ho sound, someone fucken said something about the Pope and chopping rocks and left foots and there was a fucken burble. A Catholic you say, said one of them. So that's what they look like, said another bloke. Never had a rock chopper in this fine town afore. The bushwhacker drinking beside the cove staggered to the buggy and slipped the shafts out of the harness and grabbed the simpering horse roughly by the mane and led it away, somewhere unknown beyond the main street. You won't need any horse no more, said the bully. We got special transportations around here for Catholics. Well, you wouldn't think those drunken fucks could move so quick but it was the best thing that had happened to them and the town in years, maybe fucken even forever, and they got the traveller and peeled off his suit and scraped off his long johns, this ugly emaciated naked stick man, and they took a coil of barbed wire from the supply store and they wrapped it tight around him around and around, and every time a barb pierced his skin he would scream and the men would fucken squeal with the pleasure, and they coiled it across the length of his body, fashioning a neat noose at the nape of the neck and then – and this even I have to fucken say was an inspired touch – when they got to the top of the skull they bent that barbed wire so it looked like an archbishop's hat. And then some fucken bright spark said here is the transport for Old Popey and do you know they loosed me from the neighbour yard and dragged me across, heels sliding on dirt, I did not want no fucken part – and they sat him sideways on my back and lashed him on with wire around my belly, and the traveller all fucken groaning and grovelling, words sliding out the side of his maw like spit, then they kicked my arse and cracked a whip and some drinkfucked drunken fuck maybe that mad uncle fired a shot over the top of us and I went skittering out of town, past the saddlery, past the grain store, past the cathouse, past Poverty Row, past the creek, past the boneyard, past One Tree Hill, past the station and its rude fucken stockyards, past any known terrain, past the afternoon, past the sundown, past the bend of the big river, past the thick eucalypt forest, past exhaustion. And then I lay fucken down.

What did the Catholic bloke say?

He didn't say anyfuckenthing, numbdick. He was dead as a maggot. I rolled over and tried to dislodge him but all he did was tumble about, caked blood and barbed wire and slack face. I slaved at trying to loose the stays with my hooves, but as you might have fucken noticed we goats lack opposable fucken thumbs. Fuck. In the end I had to roll back the other way to try to get him positioned on my back, that packet of suppurating wire-bound meat. I collapsed into some goat coma and when I woke up it might have been three fucken days later, woken by the buzz-saw whine of blowflies, millions of blowies, spilling off the rotting meat sack and into my eyes. Try rubbing blowies out of your eyes with hooves, fuck you. I had some strength back and started to walk, or limp, cinched underneath the foul rotting carcass, fly blown, fly bitten, walked onward, walked in any direction, stinking to fucken hell. I walked through a day and a night, hallucinating from the stench and the weight and the fly sound and the wire barbs biting at every stride. The next day I decided to just sit and wait and die. I found a tree being used as a corner post for a hay paddock. Not palatial, but as a death site it was as good, clearly, as fucken any. I closed my eyes, tried to focus on my fucken breathing, zen stuff, just the feel of the breath spilling over the whiskers on my upper lip, staying in that breath and nowhere else. And I realized what was going on.

And what was that?

Not the Lamb of God, just goat born of goat, carrying the sins of the world and the sins of the goat race, burdened endlessly and needlessly by traumas of the fucken past, labouring forever under the traumas and terrors that are long gone, that should be no more than shadows, but that live fat and furious in the forward consciousness. I should have jettisoned that dead weight pun intended years earlier. I was grateful for the enlightenment, any insight is a welcome insight, but sad it had to arrive at the moment of my death. I kept focusing on my breathing, fighting heroically the distraction of the blowfly torture, it was a fair moment to let go and accept the end and so I let go, and waited, and then nothingness did not arrive. Nothing did. I noticed the surge of irritation, observed it as if a neutral in this otherwise charged situation, made a careful scan of my body, observing the way my legs and belly and rump sank into the not-so-good earth, redoubled efforts on mindful breathing, but all for fucken nothing. Instead of accepting death passively and gratefully, I started to urge it and demand it. There was no peace in this fucken valley of death. Most fucken exasperating. I started rolling side to side, dislodging the black cumulus of blowflies, making the barbed wire score my back hide, budging the deteriorating corpse side to side down either flank. And perhaps it was this movement that caught the eye of the farmer. A man came over with his son, and they saw me and saw the body and shouted and then whispered and approached me with one hand outstretched as if I needed fucken mollifying, and then the man sent his son to get tinsnips and in this scenario saturated with impossibility he cut the fucken bonds from around my girth, and the carcass mummied in barbed wire fell from my back and I wobbled upright, beaten bad but unburdened. And you know how I rewarded that kind farmer?

You stayed with them and became a faithful goat retainer?

No, I hammered off as deep as I could into the fucken bush and never trusted a fucken human from that day to this. You are weird animals. Whether you fucken admit it or not. Just the hot dead pressure of existence and eternity.

I had not moved for the duration of the goat's story, and now I was sore again from the compacted sand bed. I checked the position of the sun and stretched and brushed myself off and then lay down all over again. Nowhere to go. No other way to be. No no nothing.

What about fucken you, said the goat, looking balefully in my direction.

I really have nothing to tell. The past is of no interest to me; my life has never been happier since I developed this goldfish brain. Every ten seconds, everything, new again. In truth, the past is of no interest to me; my life has never been happier since I developed this goldfish brain. Every ten seconds, everything, new again.

Droll, said Grim.

Every ten seconds, everything, new again.

That cabbage is no sweeter triple fucking boiled.

I had a very strange experience on my walk. I think the brain can do things we don't know it can do, but that is no great revelation for anyone who has had mental illness.

Again with the fucken mental illness, said the goat.

Well, I could tell you instead about my faithful companion, chronic pain, if you prefer. It is there in bad times as well as good. It asks nothing except to be noticed, constantly. If it ever absents itself, it will not be gone long. Auf Wiedersehen, never goodbye. It is a rare constant in a life of flux. I ache until my eyeballs sweat, then I have a little spell, but the aching never actually goes away. It is just buried temporarily beneath the louder squawk of other hurts. But you can still hear it if you listen. I know you think you deserve something significant to match your own At Death's Door sharing. I haven't got much. I recall that in the early years of primary school I consoled myself in bed each night with a fantasy about having one leg. It may have been, technically, apotemnophilia, but the point was not the act of amputation but the desirable life that would follow. I would have a peg leg, or just a stump; I would have crutches, or

I would crawl. The point always seemed to be that people would treat me kindly and make allowances for me. But it was always the leg – not blindness or any other infirmity. There are fault lines that run through the lives of a lot of men; one is in late adolescence; another is middle-age. If I'm special it's maybe just that I started early on those pains.

Fucken marvellous, said the goat. What the fuck does it have to do with us?

I read about Joe Grim when I was little. He was always in lists of indomitable boxers, and I wanted more than anything to grow into a man who could not be hurt by others. Joe Grim was that dream.

It is not quite the way you might think it is, said Grim.

I'm sure, I said.

Fucken same for me, said the goat.

I don't care, I said.

Cast your eye around, said the goat, and you see rocks that might be lumps of fucken gold or silver or uranium or plutonium or dirt-bound constellations of rubies and sapphires, and what is the fucken use. All these elements that raise insane prices on the international mineral market, and you wouldn't fucken give tuppence for any fucken one of them just now. But half a bucket of humble dihydrogen monoxide would be worth any price. Irony of ironies.

I have no idea what you are on about, I said.

Then you went to the wrong place of learning, said the fucken goat. You should have got a decent education. People like you: a pestilence of ignorance. I'll give you a clue: it exists in all three fucken physical states. It just doesn't exist inside my mouth right now.

Foul beast. I was thirsty and hungry and bereft, with sand granules caked around my nostrils and the edges of my eyes and the seams of my body where I had been moist from heat but where there was now just dry. But worse than all, worse even than the thirst, was the waiting. The nothing to do and the nowhere to go.

Grim was silent, staring somewhere past the horizon. I looked at his idiosyncratic mug. The nose was long and slant and moved off course when he shook his head, a grotesque pygostyle. His brow was impastoed with myriad lumps and ridges, skin splits knitted but not disappeared, the rugged topography a history text of leather-clad fists impacting from innumerable angles, and doubtless sharp elbows and head-butts as well. His hair was thick and oily. Both ears were badly cauliflowered. [32]

I beckoned the goat and it grumpily assented and plodded to my side. From this vantage I could see the scars beneath the short hair on its back and flanks, an orgy of rips and tears and healed wounds. Maybe that barbed-wire story had been true after all. The thing that always strikes me, I said to the goat, is that a body can bear so much damage, and then at that very last moment of life – or just after in fact: the first moment of death – it all adds to nought. No matter how smashed your flesh vehicle might be, how denuded or ablated or corrupted or excoriated, from that first moment of death onward you are in the same position as the person with the silky effortless untrammelled body who also just died. We eke every last year and minute from our bodies and we curse for this or fret for that, and then it is over and the most beautiful, the most hideous, the most physically ept or incpt, every dead body is the same.

I am addled by the fucken thought that this could be any kind of fucken revelation for you.

---

32 Information best kept from Dr. J. F. G. Pietersen of Ashwood House, Kingswinford, near Dudley, Stafford, member of the Medico-Psychological Association of Great Britain and Ireland from 1888 onward, who described, 'An effusion of blood or of bloody serum between the cartilage of the ear and its perichondrium, occurring in certain forms of insanity and sometimes among the sane,' with cauliflower ears tending to be 'worse in those forms of insanity in which the mental excitement runs high for any length of time.'

By the time Grim dies, his body will have swallowed one hundred thousand blows. Is all that concussive energy still going to be inside him, absorbed into his body, or does it get released when he expires, or has it already been absorbed into the ground or the air or the universe? Where does that trove of pain sluice off to? Where does any pain in the world end up?[33] Does it disappear when someone dies, or does the pain live on, seeking a new host, the first law of pain thermodynamics? Does Grim carry those punches tattooed just a millimetre or two below the skin, subcutaneous renderings of the bludgeoning, or do the power and the hurt and the sickening sounds of contact diffuse like morning mist and live only in the memory of hack sportswriters or those spectators not too boozed to remember the atrocity they witnessed? If he is punched in the head one hundred times, would another ten blows matter, when, if you took any rational man and smashed him ten times in his noggin, he would be livid, or wounded, or dead? Does the sensation Grim feels when he is punched in the face bear any relationship to what you feel, or I feel; actually, just what I feel, because you are a goat and idiot-insensible, but how can I know that what he calls pain is experienced as identical or even similar to what I call pain?

These are inane fucken questions, charming maybe from a small child, leadenly predictable for a beginning philosophy student, and risible from one such as yourfuckenself. There is a thing called courtesy: that can mean doing the reading and finding out the accepted wisdom before opening your mouth and styling yourself as wide-eyed truth seeker when in fact you are just too lazy to ascertain what better thinkers have postulated. But the short answer is: yes.

Yes?

Sorry, said the goat. I meant to say fucken yes.

---

33 'Now I know: All pain is the same. Only the details are different.' Kevin Powers, *The Yellow Birds*

Grim's cheeks were a beautiful dark goldenrod, skin so smooth it looked almost delicate: as if you could blow on it and it would riffle. His neck was strong, wide at the base where it met well-developed trapezoids, which truncated at narrow shoulders. Arms steely but slender. His most distinctive feature, apart from the globule nose that sat like a sac of fat, was the long jawline that descended at almost exactly a forty-five degree angle from the base of each mangled ear. His chest was hard and hairless, small nipples, with a little knot beneath the skin above the xiphoid process.

I guess this a good place to die, Grim said.

I don't know if this is a good place to die. I thought you might want to die in Italy or at least Philadelphia.

I've appeared in nicer venues, Grim said. A bit sorry not to sell tickets, but so it goes. Really don't think it is going to be long now. Probably just after sundown. So if it's all the same to you I might sit here quietly and reflect a little longer.

The goat simpered and looked grave and irritating.

I grumbled and twisted to try to find greater comfort in the rough sand ditch. Tuned out, somehow, and when I paid attention again I wondered if Grim and the goat were dead, but presumably they were sleeping. Then I thought possibly I was dead but I could smell the goat and feel the weight of the sand filling my eye cavities and flesh folds, and that sensory information probably is not available in the after realm. The sun was down, but the air was hardly less hot. I watched the stars start to bleed into apparentness in the broad blackblue baize. The goat farted, so it was still alive. Grim's knotty forehead was knitted as if he was concentrating hard on something he had just forgotten. I shuffled my filthy body in the sand. I had thought, truly, that the end would come packaged with a liminal buffer of benign diminuendo, some soft pacific anaesthetized fading, and then lights out. But it was not like that. I was irritable restless inside my body and listless irritable in my head, and time stalled then raced then stalled and it was not the least bit pleasant.

And then I closed my eyes and waited.

And then time[34] started to pass.

And then, eyes involuntarily open, I saw the stars all properly bright and spangly.

And I reclosed my eyes and let it all wash through.

---

34 'As if time wasn't muddy, silted, swept-up dust all scribbling into liquid.'
    Jennifer Mills, *Dyschronia*

15.

And you didn't die, I said.

We didn't die.

How were you rescued?

That's probably the wrong question. But we were freed from that prison of endless open desert, and we proceeded to Western Australia.

Did you keep riding the goat?

The goat became absent at some point. Mercifully. Now that yarn has given me quite the thirst. Do you think you could nip out for another flagon of this good nectar? Those royals certainly know their sherry.

16.

A different day.

What's up, my uncle said.

I sat down. I didn't look at him. I just said, It hasn't been an easy time. There was this mad dog howling at the gate and I realized far too late that it was me. Such a noisy dog. Such a *silly* dog. Howl at anything, howl at the wrong things, howl at the wrong times. And frightening, too – scares me half to death, and even once I worked out who the howling dog actually is, it didn't make it much less frightening.

Thought about trying to make friends with the dog?

I expected you'd have something more interesting than that, I said. That stuff, I can get for a buck a cliché at my local homily dispenser. If the dog is so desperate to be friends, maybe it could be friends with the worm. You're supposed to say what worm, and I reply that it's the malevolent fat worm that lives in my brain. It lies dormant most of the time, not stirring for months or occasionally years on end. And then it whips into action, comes alive with a vigour unmatched by anything else that lives inside my skull, and bores its way through otherwise reasonable thought patterns, flexing its fat body and exulting in the damage it causes, the wanton, mindless mind damage. And while I hate that worm and hate what it does, the greater problem, I sometimes think, is the simple dumb dread of knowing that he's there but not knowing when he will awake. The way, every day, he kicks my arse through the fear I have that he might arc up again. Viewed backwards, of course, I can clearly see that there are long scads of time where the worm does nothing, just sleeps fat and fallow in some back room of my skull. But this means nothing. If you flip a coin and throw ninety-nine heads in a row, there is no guarantee that the next throw will be a head – or indeed a tail. And just because I go long stretches of time with the worm neutered by fetid slumber does not mean it won't wake and ream holes in my mind patterns today, or that he won't do it for the next umpteen days in sequence. He is as powerful as he is ugly. I hate that hideous fat worm.

So I shouldn't suggest you make friends with the worm.

Other people can do what they want with their worms, if they've got them. I will continue with my time-tested method of just splashing about in the warm worm-flavoured waters of self-pity. Occasionally howling.

17.

My uncle riffling papers, shuffling them front to back, tossing discards over his shoulder, searching for something in the teetering paper stacks.

You're still interested in Grim, he said. I've been thinking, and reading, and remembering – the last one is the hardest part. It is conceivable that Grim suffered – if that is the right word, and it probably isn't – from pain asymbolia. In this condition, usually related to brain injury, cingulotomy, morphine analgesia or lobotomy, the sensation of pain is experienced without unpleasantness. If this had been Grim's condition, that should have been uncovered by the medical tests he underwent early in his career. It seems more likely that pain was simply something Grim went through, and for which he had a phenomenally high level of forbearance.

If you have a look here – waving a fly-specked paperback – T. O. Beidelman argues[35] that pain is related to imagination. We can construct an idea of Grim as a man of such limited imagination that he cannot – or, perhaps more correctly, does not – think what might happen next. Or he assumes correctly that the next thing that happens to him will be another punch in the face, but he cannot imagine that this will lead to long-term damage. Or he does not imagine the hideous thoughts and desires of the most bloodthirsty spectators, or the vicious longings of his opponent, all of which helps inoculate him against the leaps of imagination that would render the pain sensations intolerable.

So if that is true, I said, struggling to follow, it suggests Grim had little or no empathy.

---

35 *The Cool Knife*

My uncle tossed aside Beidelman and picked up a newer volume. Rubbed the cover clean on the front of his shirt. This book was recommended to me by a murderer, he said. True story. With the empathy question, contrarily, I think the Grim opponent was disadvantaged if he was 'vulnerable' to feeling empathy – an attribute Michel Foucault in this difficult book[36] suggested was part of the invention of Man that occurred at the Enlightenment. Foucault pushed this idea further to argue that empathy for other humans means pain inflicted on a punished person also causes pain to the punisher. Was this the experience[37] of Grim's opponents, not just bruising their fists on the head and body of this infernal man but hurting their hearts and souls as well? It must have been confounding to find oneself unable to knock Grim out and simultaneously unable to prevail in the weird supra-contest Grim constructed, but did this inversion mean it felt less like sport and more like a nightmare? Did it seem, after a time, as if one was committing a criminal act, inflicting violence on a victim unable to respond in kind?

Perhaps it was a bully's dream. Perhaps some opponents enjoyed it enormously.

You must not forget that there was always a third person in the ring, but the role of the referee was neutered by Grim's resilience. The crowd had paid, quite explicitly, to come and see if Grim could endure the beating, and no referee had the imprimatur to stop that fun. There was only a minimal chance[38] that Grim would win, so

---

36 *Discipline and Punish*

37 "'But if we follow that theory,' I said, 'shouldn't the fellow who does the laughing be the one who throws the punch, not the one who catches it?'
    "'It's not that simple,' Beth insisted. 'Maybe the guy who gets hurt laughs to hang on to his superiority ... '" Budd Schulberg, *The Harder They Fall*

38 Grim won a 'newspaper decision' against the hapless Jack Daly (career: seven fights, zero wins) at the Keystone Athletic Club, Philadelphia, in

the referee's role was reduced to waving entrée to permitted action at the start of each round and pushing the combatants apart when they clinched too long; a glorified usher, tepidly humiliated before the throng by insignificance he did not anticipate.

Meanwhile Grim kept turning up, kept swallowing all of the cruelty that leather-bound fists could administer.

You will be thinking that possibly he found the pain enriching on a spiritual level.

I had considered it.

Ariel Glucklich in this curious tome[39] writes of pain's transformative power, that 'the self as a phenomenal organization of perceptions, motivations, commands and actions emerges out of the violence and out of the hurtful feedback it generates.' Glucklich speculates[40] that 'a pain-induced subservience to a greater telos turns the torture into a ritual of self-sacrifice.' Perhaps this is the jag that Grim was on.

Maybe.

But I don't think so. I think he had a particular talent, and he was just earning money, and he was doing what he did, and getting through it all.

February 1908 – the same year he travelled to Australia – but did not win any of his next thirty-one fights, as listed by BoxRec.

39 *Sacred Pain: Hurting the Body for the Sake of the Soul*

40 Specifically in relation to Native American piercing, but extrapolation can be made.

18.

In the weather-beaten weatherboard church in Norguna the sermon elongates like a wire maker spinning a length of wire, longer and thinner, longer and thinner, until it seems impossible that it will keep going, but it does. The sermon stretching beyond clock time and entering calendar time, then geological time, then space time, then no time at all. The church sweating, the wooden pews opening their pores, squeezing out globules of old wood sweat. Stained glass windows swaying in the heat, sagging in the window frames, the timbers of the wall slumping, the sermon rolling on, on. Grim can smell the moisture coming through the wool of his suit. The dirt is emptying from under his fingernails, washed out by sweat. His bones have softened. His lungs are water.

The only way he can keep alive is to focus, very deeply, very sharply, on the neck of Mrs. Etteridge in the pew in front. She has inclined her body in the pew in such a way that the fat of her upper back flows over the top of the seat. She is wearing a dress the colour of prunus blossom. Her hat is old and the colour of a blood plum. It has a raggedy tail of lace netting. Grim guesses that if he sucked it, it would taste of dust and cotton and head sweat. Her hair is matted like the pelt of a baby rabbit. Below the hairline and above her collar is a neck made of horizontally stacked rolls of flesh. When she drops her chin to her chest in prayer, and eyes are supposed to be closed, Grim is intrigued by the horizontal lines that appear as the fat rolls elongate. Sweat is creeping through the fabric of her dress. He pretends to study the front of the hymn book and leans his head far forward until his face is inches from her neck. He feels suspended, doesn't want to move nearer or further away. He breathes in surreptitiously. He closes his eyes and leans back in his pew and tries to think other thoughts. The minister's voice is dry as a Methodist wine tasting. Grim thinks of the last Protestant service he attended, a shipboard burial, and the quotidian mundanity of the words uttered, so far from the numinous Latin arcana of his own church: like seeing a royal parlour furnished with objects made of unvarnished hardwood. As he was struggling into consciousness in the Norguna cemetery he heard a bell and assumed it was some sort of summons and found himself stumbling to the town's lone church. Not unhappy to be here, merely confused. Eyes falling in and out of focus. Tendrils of sweat hurrying down his calves and the narrow of his back. He runs his hands over his cheeks and wipes them dry on his trousers. Her neck. Her damp hair. When he was a teen touting for shoeshine work in Philadelphia, there were muttered conversations with other bootblacks; the code word they used was 'polishing,' and they explained to him and even demonstrated how it was done, greasy hands pummelling their pale privates for a few quick jerks and then the ludicrous pearlescent squirting; but it was not something that he could do. Not possible. Instead he slogged about, supersaturated with turbid obsessions: this girl's fur coat cuffs, that woman's dark and wide eyebrows, the piscine eyes of a dark girl glimpsed outside the market, loose braided hair, a certain timbre, quarter-smiles: these like priceless artworks in the gallery of himself that he would peruse again and again every nighttime, fevered with the impossibility of release, and somehow this made ever speaking to any female he encountered in daylight more impossible. Leaning forward again, swooning toward Mrs. Etteridge, that peculiar nausea, and for a microsecond, just, his tongue emerges quick as a gecko and he laps the moisture from the back of her neck, a single darting upsweep, and she stiffens, and then her hand comes up to feel the place where his tongue was moments before, but she does not turn her head, and Grim sinks back and screws his eyes tight closed, and no one says a word and perhaps nothing was noticed or known, and the sermon trudges on.

He tastes her salts on his tongue. Can still smell the moist hair, her aroma inside his nostrils. He tries to relax his jaw, his shoulders, his mind. Staring at the cross high on the forward wall. There is no question that he could have breezed through the whipping and the scourging, would not have flinched as the thorns in the crude crown punctured his scalp, perhaps could have stood the hammering of the huge square-headed nails through his wrists and his ankles. But what then? Could he have borne the crucifixion any better than Christ did? He thinks on it, tongue running around the outside of his lips as he tries to calculate the weight of the agony, factoring in the brutes breaking Jesus's legs, and piercing his side, and the length of time there with all of his broken body collapsing against those three shocking metal spikes. And he decides that no, if Christ could not, he could not. He thinks of the jeering from the goons below the cross. He is used to this; he would hear every word and not care. But he does not think he could withstand what Christ could not withstand – although, always that nagging disappointment that as the end neared, Jesus gave his tormentors the satisfaction of hearing him scream out his despair. INRI. Grim thinks about this. He thinks he would have said other things. Many other things. He thinks of the men who were crucified upside down, and wonders if that discombobulation actually made the entire torment slightly easier to bear, rather than harder; he remembers sections of fights with his brain scrambled into slop, and how he could notice but not feel the blows that hit him through that time. He thinks of men ensnared in underground torture chambers, and the probability that he could stand the physical torments, and the near certainty that the torturers would devise other personalized horrors that would work on him with great and precise effectiveness. Then he thinks of the baby Jesus, there amongst the farm animals, plump and delicate and perfect. Grim loves baby Jesus, and always has. He prefers to think about baby Jesus more than any other aspect of the whole Biblical carnival. Snug and loved, the drama not yet begun. He decides not to think about crucifixion or torture anymore.

The trifold amen sung in a dry gargle to close the service. Exiting to the sunblasted morning, hand pumped by the parson: hair the colour of sand, cheeks florid, white dog collar, mouth downturned at the corners. Good morning, he effused, good to see you. New in Norguna?

Yup.

Well, welcome. Can we expect to worship with you again?

The Roman Catholics, do they have a church here?

Oh. No, we have the town's only church. If you're Roman, you will be wanting the next town along.

Bene.

A dry husk of a church service. Not much ritual, no Latin, no magic. Grim was reminded, by way of absurd comparison, of the far distant cathedral in Avellino, which led back to memories of home, and of his brother, and of his mother, and felt simultaneously closer to all that and even further away. You could suck on that dry protestant husk all day and never get a drop of spiritual relief. He remained on the hook, surly. And then he thought about the National Shrine of Saint Rita of Cascia that was built near the intersection of South Broad and Ellsworth in Philly, the exact corner where he worked as a bootblack when he was first off the boat in the U.S.A. Rita of Cascia, patron saint of wounds, patron saint of abuse, patron saint of impossible causes. They finished the shrine just before he left on the long journey to Australia. He climbed the fifteen steps. Ran his hands over the dark wooden doors. Thought about Avellino. Thought about Gio. Muttered a prayer and left.

Grim noticed several of the women in their small hats turning their gaze his way, perhaps parsing his eligibility. Mrs. Etteridge was one. He ignored them and strode the short block to the town's main street. Nothing uncommon to witness there – a couple of stores, a public hall, long troughs for watering horses, two pubs, a vacant corner waiting for war to break out so that it could be fitted with a bathetic statue. He would never know the things that all small-town people know about their own small towns – in the case of Norguna, for example, every person knew that two days earlier Herbert Oakey was caught lying beneath the slats of the verandah in front of the grocer's store. Mrs. Baddinton spotted him and yelled; he was trying to spy up women's skirts. Dick Baddinton dragged Oakey out by the feet and rinsed his eyes with urine, right there on the main street. Everyone laughed. But now that story is town folklore, which means only those who live there can know it.

19.

I was talking with my wife and my son, I said to my uncle, and my wife said what are you working on, but you know it's okay if you are not telling me. We have been together a lot of years and she knows that I am cactus prickly about discussing what I'm writing until it's written. And my son said it's the exploded non-fiction novel with Grim and the goat, and my wife said I'm not sure if that is a real answer or you're just joking. My son said real and she said what is an exploded non-fiction novel and I told her and she said okay, good for you. I asked my son how he knew about what I was working on and he said you keep telling me and I said really, do I, I don't remember ever talking about this at all. And he shook his head. And now a parenthetical thought: earlier that day I was thinking how my biggest hero through most of childhood was Ned Kelly, and doubtless a large part of his attractiveness was his imperviousness to pain via armour to keep out slings and arrows and whips and scorns, and then when I was older, in fact a late teen, I was entrapped by the persona of his best friend, Joe Byrne, a brittle and human counterpoint to the impossible ultra-masculine ideal of Ned, and then when I was mad at one time and researching them I thought for a while I might indeed be Joe Byrne, which would have been hard given that he died a century before I was born, but madness [41] gets around these inconveniences, and then I wrote a play at one point that no one ever wanted to stage that was called

---

41   When Robert Lowell was lost in his madness, he imagined on various occasions that he was Napoleon, Hitler, John the Baptist, Dante, Milton, and, among others, of course, Christ. Lowell was also a deeply flawed human. But he wrote 'Skunk Hour' and 'Memories of West Street and Lepke.'

Save Me, Joe Byrne. The title was a borrow from the story of a young African-American man being put to death in a U.S. prison and as the poison gas entered the execution chamber they could hear him incanting over and over, 'Save me, Joe Louis,' and vulnerable young men I think have always hoped for a more powerful male to intercede in their fate at the last minute. End of parentheses. For some reason then I thought of all the projects I have worked on and not told my wife the details of until they were done, and all of them coming to nought: the novels, unpublished, unwanted; the plays, unproduced, unwanted; innumerable poems, reviews, monologues, opinion columns, soiled rags of on-spec journalism, and, of course, indigestible short stories, perhaps my most awful metier, actually obviously not, that would definitely be the poetry. And I tried to do some math, and I thought it might be between half a million and a million words written in hope of publication and then thrown back in my face or, far more accurately, slumping slowly into the void of non-acknowledgement. And I tried and failed to convert those words (most redrafted-rethought-rewritten three, five, seventeen times) into minutes and days and I could not do it, and then I realized that what they added up to, really, was most of a lifetime. And I said to my wife, I have spent my allotted years [42] in a room alone writing words no one wants or will ever read, it is the most stupid life imaginable. And my wife, my perfect wife, held me tight against her in my wretchedness and said, No, darling; it might be absurd, but it is not stupid.

You deserve such a wife, my uncle said.

---

42 Not, as it happens, a unique viewpoint.
    'What have I been doing all my life? Have I been idle, or have I nothing to shew for all my labour and pains? Or have I passed my time in pouring words like water into empty sieves, rolling a stone up a hill and then down again, trying to prove an argument in the teeth of facts, and looking for causes in the dark, and not finding them?' William Hazlitt, 'The Indian Jugglers'

I should have spent those years just watching her, watching the way she moves through rooms, watching the way she bends to a task, watching how she negotiates the world and the people within it and smooths out ripples and improves moments without flash or noise or ego. That would have been an instructive use of a lifetime.

No, not stupid: just absurd.

There was silence in the dusty room for a time and then the wheezing of my uncle as he dug into the pile, searching for a title, tossing books north and south. And then, finally, he found Thea Astley's *Drylands* and turned the pages carefully and then handed it across. The awful realization made by the author character Janet Deakin, he said. Read this.

'She couldn't stop. It was the pointlessness of it all … The idiocy of her wasted years made her laugh even more.'

20.

Norguna, the main street leached of colour by the sharpened sunrays and the patina of dust.

I'm intrigued by the men who fought you in the ring, I said.

I made them plenty of money, Grim said.

I think they lacked imagination. I could have beaten you.

Beating me wasn't their problem.

No, I think I could have defeated you. Stopped you.

No one can knock Joe Grim out. That is everything.

But that was all they tried. I would do something different.

An iron bar? A cosh wrapped in an old handkerchief?

No. I would not hit you.

What would you do?

I don't know. But I would not do what you expected. I would run away from you. Try to make you mad. Force you to do the hitting, not the being hit.

The crowd would riot.

Let them. I would run backwards round and round the ring, and Joe Grim would be dumbfounded and forced into being the attacker for once, and you would be confused and get heavy-legged from the chasing and tired from trying to punch, and angry at the lack of respect.

The worst disrespect: not trying to knock Joe Grim out.

What would happen?

A lot of people would want their money back, a lot of bottles would be thrown at us in the ring, the police would have to stop the event and take us away for our own safety. I don't think it's your best idea.

I think it's all right.

That is because you live in your head and not your body. You live on a page and not amongst humans. You exist in Pretendland.

Yeah, I said. Also, Joe, I was thinking of the masochist and the sadist.

Yes?

The masochist said: Hit me. And the sadist said: No.

21.

I'm intrigued by my uncle perched at the base of the western wall of words, ancient forefinger tracking down an early page[43] in the palindromic Mark Kram's masterpiece on Ali-Frazier III, while in his other hand he had a dusty typescript, a few pages of scribbled notes, and a Roland Barthes tome.

You took your time, he said, jerking his head toward his teacup. Do I look like a camel? This remembering is thirsty damn work.

Fair enough, I said, replenishing his cup. What were we talking about earlier?

You were telling me that your life has been decades of writing words no one wants.

Why do you think that is?

You know why. It's because you only ever pretend to write to anyone else. You have spent a life writing only to yourself.

That's a bitter pill, I said. Perhaps we can return to Grim.

Ignoring is as good a strategy as forgetting, my uncle said. But whatever. Well – we've magically moved from the desert to a little town in Western Australia, with the scene set via an improbable country church interlude that owes much to the author's upbringing and considerably less to narrative fidelity. We were going overland toward Perth for Grim's fight over there, a crazy journey for modest pay. And it's coming to me now: sitting on a seat outside the Norguna stock and station agency. Grim was wondering why I was staring into space. I couldn't help him with that; I don't think I knew why, myself. He picked up several neatly typed pages that were fluttering through the morning and fetched up against our seat. He read

---

43   ' ... in a tenuous self, boxing was still irreducible.' Mark Kram, *Ghosts of Manila*

them quickly, a feat of some awkward surprise for the exploded non-fiction novelist because it is difficult to gauge when and where he could have become literate in English, but it would be still less credible if the sheets had been scribbled in Italian. He pushed the sheaf toward me, breaking my reverie. It's titled 'Instructive Incident at Upstate California Lumber Camp,' he said. Nice stuff. It says at the top that you wrote it when you were about twenty-two and then lost it for a long time and realized on rediscovering it how the same old concerns have always been there but also the same inability to crest the hill, to move from competent sentences to prose with meaning and value. Oh that, I said. Nothing ever new; these neural schemata are deep grooves. Show me the story, because honestly I do not recall ever writing such a thing, but that is not uncommon.

22.

Instructive Incident at Upstate California Lumber Camp

Saitchell, he was a strong man. Strong! Christ. I've known men like him, who never said much but other men were always careful to nod their way. Everyone knew. A farmer, I think it was Collie Rogers or at least his brother; I saw him once hold the hind leg of a heifer with his right arm and milk her with his left; the heifer had been kicking pails and playing up for his girl, so Collie (or his brother) took over. Calm, no fuss. So strong. And Saitchell was of that stripe, the strongest man in the lumber camp, maybe the strongest in California or so it seemed.

Saitchell has been ridden hard though by Lonnie McVitty. McVitty, big and dark, with a streak of nastiness like shit through a shrimp. Saitchell is ten or maybe even fifteen years older than McVitty, three inches shorter. The gang boss keeps them apart. But McVitty has said something, which he usually does, and this time it has stung Saitchell. He's carting it with him like a burr in his boot.

Jimmy told me that McVitty was boasting about this and that down by the quarter-mile marker at knock-off yesterday. Then he got to talking about men who were past it, who should go to the coast and find soft jobs. No names mentioned but you could guess who he was needling. Saitchell thought it was a putdown, anyway. He picked up his scoring axe and made ten blows, fast as wingbeats, in descending order down a trunk. Measure 'em, he said.

Curse my eyes if they didn't measure out almost exactly: seven inches apart, seven inches, seven and an eighth, seven, seven, six and fif-sixteenths, seven, seven – all the rest sevens. There were mutterings of approval, or wonder, then McVitty unhinges his jaw and says, Parlour game trick, Saitchell. Pretty.

That's what he says. You look at the words themselves and you don't see what is so wrong, but Saitchell knew what he meant. Saitchell didn't need it spelled for him.

You're a blowhard, he tells McVitty.

There's a problem, old man?

Piss and wind. Oughta keep your flap shut.

And you'll make me shut it?

Someone says, Quit it up, boys, and someone else tells that someone to bag it, because we can all see it's getting interesting.

You want to take a pop? That's McVitty again, goading him.

I'm not going to break my hand on your worthless skull.

You're going cur in your old age. So just don't talk no more.

No, not a cur, says Saitchell. You want to settle this, we'll do it the proper way.

No one knows what the proper way is. It looks like Saitchell might point of fact be backing down; McVitty is starting to preen, he's doing jokes and loud laughs with his crony Hadley and inviting the Smith brothers and Larsson to join in, too, but they all keep watching. Saitchell talks to Auld Father and he shrugs and then nods and then pulls aside McVitty and he doesn't look a bit happy but in the end he nods his head. Auld Father limps off to the hut and we are all standing there slapping at legs and arms to stay warm. Then Saitchell says how it's going to be and there is a cheer because this is an unanticipated treat and we follow in clumps to the cookhouse like excited sprogs on Christmas morning.

Auld Father has taken two pokers from the bunk hut and rested them in either end of the kitchen fire. He explains the rules: once the pokers are hot enough, Saitchell and McVitty will take one each and at the count press the tip onto the opposing man's skin. The first to flinch away is the loser. He says this is the way such things have been settled by tree-fellers since time immemorial and no one is old enough to challenge him on it.

McVitty makes a display of removing his outerwear, then his shirt, and flexes his deep chest as he hauls off his BV. He is still booming jokes off Hadley, but the laughter sounds strained.

Saitchell is pinched and grim as he shucks his clothing. He is lean and hard, a body like Speckled Bob Fitzsimmons, but the pallor of too many forest winters greys his skin. He speaks to no one. If he was a prizefighter he would do without a corner man. I want him to win, but I fancy he would be irritated if he knew. Actually I don't truly want him to win. I want only for McVitty to lose.

How long?

Whenever you want, McVitty, says Auld Father. Whenever you and Saitchell agree.

Not until it's good and hot, Saitchell says.

The banter has subsided to almost nothing. Everyone watching, chewing on their cheeks, wondering.

That must be hot enough, says Auld Father.

The tips of the pokers are a dull crimson. Saitchell leans close to inspect them both and, apparently suspecting that one is hotter than the other, moves the left poker deeper into the fire.

Ought to use a fuck-damn branding iron, shouts McVitty. Do it properly.

Auld Father looks uncomfortable. A few of us press forward to examine the irons; the tips are now tending scarlet. You won't get white-hot in this fire, Auld Father says.

I'm in no hurry, Saitchell says.

You hoping to wait me out?

Just don't want to make it too easy, McVitty.

They are trying to jest, it seems, but no one thinks it is anything other than what it is: two bulls, one paddock.

Then the young bull loses patience. That's goddamn hot enough, shouts McVitty. Let's have at it.

Saitchell pauses, as if he is a little saddened not to wait until the poker tips are molten, then smiles a smile as hard and tight as a split wedge. He gestures to McVitty to have his choice of weapon. McVitty chooses the poker furthest from him, as if suspecting some four-flushing. He picks it up, using his shirt as a mitt. Saitchell takes the other poker and stands a little more than an arm span from his antagonist.

On my call then, Auld Father says. Three and, two and, one. Now!

Both men lift their pokers and jab them into the other's upper chest. Saitchell is grey and resolute. McVitty looks wild. The contest lasts a single heartbeat. Goddammit, McVitty screams, reeling back and hurling his poker to the floor. God damn you. He slaps at the lividity on his breast. Saitchell refuses to even touch his, and lays his weapon down with a dark scowl.

Which is where it should have ended. But someone reamed McVitty, said the contest never even got started, and what was that effort from him all about, anyway. McVitty got wilder and said, Shit on all that, I was taken by surprise. Do it again, Saitchell, you sly old creep.

And Saitchell by now is halfway out of the cookhouse, shrugging back into some clothes; there is a cherry-red patch on the top left of his body but he is pretending it doesn't exist.

I've taught you a lesson already, says Saitchell. Can't teach you more if you won't learn, you slob.

I was dog-packed. I'm ready for you this time.

You're a fool, McVitty.

Then the usual words about cowardice and running away and by the end Saitchell is back half-naked again, looking greyer than even before. The pokers are back in the fire, and McVitty is moodily staring at the point of one and then the other, trying to find an advantage. He doesn't wait for the invitation, doesn't give Saitchell the honour of choosing, but snatches one out of the embers and says, Come on then.

Saitchell picks up the other and he is looking almost sad, free arm limp, head slightly dropped forward, as Auld Father sounding impatient gives another call.

Three and, two and, one.

Before the count has finished, fractionally before, McVitty rams his poker into the front of Saitchell's shoulder. You can see he is pressing hard. Saitchell quickly returns the favour and McVitty yelps and starts to flinch but he holds on. Two seconds. Four. There is the smell of McVitty's curlicues of body hair singeing. There is a gurgling inside his throat.

Saitchell has not budged. McVitty's poker is jammed into his flesh but he stares straight back at him. Then McVitty suddenly pulls back his own poker and rams it forward again, straight into the side of Saitchell's face. Someone shouts something and someone goes to move forward and someone's arm holds him and someone else yells something else. Saitchell's eyes widen into chasms and he growls a terrible sound but he doesn't flinch backwards, even as the smouldering metal burns through his cheek and judders forward into the cavity of his mouth, and then McVitty screams his exasperation and pulls away from the torment – but leaves his own iron hanging, half in half out of Saitchell's face.

Auld Father starts to raise a hand as if to end something but his feet are nailed firm. A momentary tableau. Then Saitchell steps back a half-pace and slightly to the right and brings his poker in a glorious red arc up from near the floor into the fleshy neck below McVitty's whiskers. The big man is knocked down by the blow, a smear of colour indicating where his throat has been scorched. We look from the roaring bully on the floor to Saitchell, whose expression registers only distaste. His left cheek betrays a pulpy void. As he swiftly gathers his clothes and marches outside without even dressing, I realize that this is the most angry I have ever seen him, but feel, powerfully, that this is nowhere near the full extent of the anger in the man.

23.

Well, I said, that is – whatever it is. Never good at character names. A mention of Bob Fitzsimmons all those years ago! The familiar juddering punctuation. 'Curlicues' was a word from a Robert Lowell poem I loved at seventeen. The strong man in the first paragraph was a version of a terrifying Vietnam vet who I worked with on a farm when I was fifteen; I saw him hold the kicking leg of an angry cow with one enormous arm in the herringbone milking shed one day, and he could carry four hay bales at once, which some people don't think is a great feat: to them I say, try carrying two bales at once and see how you go. McVitty was, of course, some of the unpleasant young men I feared when I was a young man.

Who was Saitchell?

I don't know who Saitchell was. I don't know why I wrote it at twenty-two. I don't know why these peculiar obsessions endure.[44]

We are not always proud of the things that obsess us. I have always been interested in combat sports, cleaving to the moral justification that the combatants are willing and voluntary participants. The thought of children being forced to fight, such as boys shoved into special combat pits in mining areas of industrial England; or the Battle Royale for impoverished African-Americans in the U.S.A.; or men forced to kill or be killed in the Roman arena; or slaves pressed on pain of death to participate in head-butting contests – all of this shames humanity. I can hardly bear to think – quite literally – of those American brutes who grew their thumbnails long and hardened them over candles to gain a hideous advantage in gouging bouts:

---

44 'Narrative, when fetishised, can become an evolved and brilliantly disguised way of shutting our ears to what hurts and scares us the most.' Maria Tumarkin, 'This Narrated Life,' *Griffith Review*

fights in which the win was secured by scraping out an opponent's eyeball. It leaves me sickened. But I remain engrossed by the idea of powerful forbearance – Grim in the ring, or an unbreakable prisoner lugging bluestone from one corner of the punishment yard to another, as many times as required, breaking the system under the crushing weight of his stoicism. I think Grim's philosophy in its entirety – or more than a philosophy, which implies a distance between self and thought, however small; his tao, his raison d'être, his self – was simply this: I can take more punishment than they can deliver.[45] That was who he was. Or most of it, anyway.

---

45 'Suffering and human destiny are the same thing. Each is a description of the other.' Cormac McCarthy, *The Sunset Limited*

24.

You used to get newspapers sent from England? Even in 2010 there was such a thing as the internet, I said.

It's called a newspaper for a reason.

I flicked open an old *Guardian*. If you're going to push on with your story, at least make it sing, I said. Have a look at Hilary Mantel's 'Ten Rules for Writing Fiction.'[46] Number 7, in part:

> *When your character is new to a place, or things alter around them, that's the point to step back and fill in the details of their world.*

Well. Norguna smells like: animals, man sweat, vinegar, rosewater, woodsmoke, outdoor dunnies.

Norguna sounds like: birdsong, the twinkle of tack on passing horses, occasional drunken bellowing, silence.

Norguna tastes like: boiled mutton.

Norguna looks like: sun striking stone, tumbledown sheds, a full hemisphere of inscrutable sky.

Okay. Hilary Mantel's 'Ten Rules for Writing Fiction,' number 7, in different part:

> *People don't notice their everyday surroundings and daily routine, so when writers describe them it can sound as if they're trying too hard to instruct the reader.*

So perhaps I should not say: The temperature in the Norguna pub was hotter than outside, even. The humidity of man sweat and alcohol

---

46 *The Guardian*, 25 February 2010

and adrenalin. The puddle of spilled beer on the floor was veined with spider lines of spilled blood. The designation on the anteroom door was Ladies' Lounge. The all-male populace of this chamber gave that appellation the lie; perhaps the delineation was because, unlike the front bar, this room had two wall-mounted benches and a framed reproduction of a Watteau abomination covered in insect feces and hoicked phlegm.

I think you can assume Hilary would give you a gold star for that effort.

I don't know if she would like the head-butting contest or not, my not-uncle said.

What head-butting contest?

You haven't missed it; it's coming up next. The point is, it shows it's not just Grim dining at the banquet of suffering – it's lots of men. It's not just men in American lumber camps or Australian boxing tents or ancient gladiator arenas; it is also men in mining towns, and men in suburban backyards, and men in different parts of Dagestan and Sudan and Iceland and everywhere else. Something in men, in every millimetre of the world map and every dot on the line of time, desperate to scramble up that hill of pain to see how high they can get. Grim, of course, is famed for being the toughest man in the world's premier combat sport, so he should find a contest such as this in a Western Australian fly-speck town a doddle. But we already know his skull is thick; this is an opportunity to reveal something else about his character. My character is all too obvious. No one would expect me to enter such a contest, and I won't.

25.

I notice, I said to my uncle, that you are rampaging about in rural and remote Australia without ever encountering a First Nations person. I'm a little surprised.

I'm surprised you're surprised, he said. But. For what it's worth. Over time I have developed a suite of opinions about Black and white Australia, and some of them might be correct. One of those opinions is that the damage done to Indigenous people by blatant racists may be roughly equivalent to the damage done by patronizing do-gooders.[47] Another is that the whitefella lust for those things that belong to Aboriginal people knows no bounds.[48] My mob, non-Indigenous Australians, are almost crazed with desire for their art, their lore, their blessing, their music, their knowledge, access for the rapacious academic researchers who descend from every corner to probe and prod and provoke and ponder and proclaim to questionable effect, and most of all their 'Go on, forget about it' forgiveness that could ease the new and true White Man's Burden,[49] which is that we live in full knowledge that all comfort and amenity of life in this land was and is pinched from those who were here longer and here better.

And you fix that by writing a book without Aboriginal characters?

I am not comfortable as a non-Indigenous writer to invent an Aboriginal people, language, culture; but I also think it is deeply problematic for me to use people that I know and manipulate their

---

47 See, for example, Peter Sutton, *The Politics of Suffering: Indigenous Australia and the End of the Liberal Consensus*

48 See, for example, Aileen Moreton-Robinson, *Talkin' Up to the White Woman: Indigenous Women and Feminism*

49 See, for example, my essay 'The Great Red Whale.'

stories or their words for the purposes of fiction. Australians like me have stolen and continue to steal a lot from Aboriginal people, and at the very least I can avoid stealing their stories. So I avoid it, respectfully, while being aware that this becomes one more contribution to whitewashing.

What is this then, I said, selecting a crumpled piece of typescript from one of the tottering piles and shaking it in front of his face.

Ah, that. One of the early iterations of this book had a solitary Indigenous scene so as to thwart accusations of deliberate erasure, he said. It was a clever-clever passage, simultaneously twinkling its fingers toward acknowledging Indigenous primacy in this land, but through the invention of a completely bogus ceremony it also mimicked and mocked the Spooky Magic that whitefellas long for from their Aboriginal co-dependents. A certain sort of person, and you've met them, and perhaps you are one of them, will always hoist remote Aboriginal people onto the loftiest pedestal and give them unasked-for supernatural powers and tongue-bath them with platitudes,[50] while staying relaxed and comfortable that they are trapped in an economic matrix that keeps them securely at the bottom.

I assume this piece of stained and mistreated foolscap contains the scene in question?

He glanced at it.

I guess so. Just give me a paragraph of it. That is going to be enough. For everyone.

---

50   When (certain) progressive Australians make a fetish of Indigeneity, cherry-picking the Aboriginal voices they listen to and constructing Utopian fantasies of inherent Aboriginal virtue, it turns First Nations individuals into symbols – a process just as dehumanizing, ironically, as the prejudiced bullshit of racists.

Edward Said is valuable on this, demonstrating that exoticization is a product of representational systems of colonialism and imperialism.

The end, drawing closer. But then: sounds. Sticks, chanting, stomps in heavy sand. I may or may not have opened my eyes; I watched from where I was and also an epicentral position directly above the earth and the action. I was aware and watching but I did not know what Grim and goat saw or if they were alive because I could not move my head any which way; I could only see what I was there to see. The dry creek bed transformed, marked with thick lines and colour fields, highest art emblazoned on the low planes of earth itself. Black bodies moving in sequences of one, two, many, in between the colours, or observing at a side, stomping and singing and clapping wood. I reached – I could reach – and scooped a handful of the sand and from that handful I plucked out a single grain, and on that grain I saw etched the same lines and colour fields, the same design; and when I checked other grains they were all the same: the universe in each atom; the micro and the macro simultaneously. And the singing grew louder, and the dancing more insistent, and the lines and the colours more definite and transcendent, and then one group marched further down the dry sandy channel and as they marched the design continued, replicated with each footfall, until it stretched into infinitude, and then strong hands lifted me and lay me in the centre of the creek bed, and the lines and the colours went across my body, and my vision now was only of what was around me, no longer the viewpoint from above, and then I saw a row of men peel the creek bed away from the earth and start to roll it up like a rug, and I was held within the roll, and it was rolled and I was rolled, over and over, many times: and then the sensation of being lifted, and swift movement toward and through nothingness, and I let it happen, and I let it carry me, and twinkly Aboriginal fairy dust did what it does for authenticity-lusting soft white searchers, and I was vanished and reanimated and placed gently far distant elsewhere. [Still white, still privileged, still a squatter on stolen land. But within the town of Norguna a few hundred miles from Perth, Western Australia. Grim was nearby, snoring. If he could sleep there, so should I. I slept. We both did. In the dulcet desert night. Blessed blackness.]

Oh yeah, that was part of the scene. I remember writing that. Throw some fairy dust in the eyes of non-Indigenous readers and they will think you really know something because they are convinced that this is somewhere that you can really know anything. It works every time. Voila.

26.

Books opened at random. Screeds scrawled on scraps of ivory note-paper. A welter of words. A tsunami. A laboriousness. A light year.

His face was a gory mess and he stumbled forward to receive more blows, a broken and battered hull of a man foundering on a sea of pain, relentlessly buffeted by the angry waves of blows, and borne up only by some unknown fund of pointless endurance.'
– Budd Schulberg, *The Harder They Fall*

In 1833, he [James 'Deaf' Burke] fought Simon Byrne, a contender from Ireland. As the fight wore on, blood poured from Burke's ear which Byrne had bitten, almost severing it from his head. After over three hours of bare-knuckle, ear-bit-ing mayhem, Byrne lay on the ground and conceded defeat. Byrne died shortly afterward and Burke went to trial for his murder. The jury found Burke not guilty based on the testimony of a surgeon who suggested that other factors, in addition to the boxing match, might have contributed to Byrne's death. Ironically, Byrne had killed an opponent in the ring in 1830 and barely escaped the hangman's noose with a verdict of not guilty, thus making Byrne one of only a handful of fighters with the dubious honor of involvement in boxing deaths both as accused murderer and victim.
– Christopher David Thrasher, *Fight Sports and American Masculinity: Salvation in Violence from 1607 to the Present*

In the taxonomy of violence, the formal duel resided at the apex of the pyramid. Next came semi-institutionalized combat at militia musters, court days, huskings, and celebration days.

Slickings stood somewhere in the middle of the pyramid. Individual outbursts of rage such as cowhidings, horsewhippings, and canings were further down. These temper tantrums were generally regarded as legitimate acts of violence since the perpetrator usually employed them against individuals who had insulted a gentleman but who were not considered of a high enough social rank to warrant a challenge. The base of the pyramid of violence consisted of noninstitutional forms of mayhem such as knifings, back-alley brawls, blackguardings, and fisticuffs – the latter two being the common man's way of defending honor. They were also unfortunately replete with eye gouging and ear biting. Many 'maimed faces' with mutilated ears and noses, bore witness to the general level of mayhem. A particularly dexterous fellow, for example, could pluck an opponent's eyeballs from their sockets with one good thrust of the thumbs.
– Dick Steward, *Duels and the Roots of Violence in Missouri*

[M]asculinity isn't always a pleasant thing to behold, and it's always difficult, sometimes unpleasant to write about – it's certainly a difficult thing in just about every respect.
– Paul Smith, *Boys: Masculinities in Contemporary Culture*

27.

My town,[51] in the years I was growing up[52] there, had nine hundred and something people – the number wavered, but it never reached four figures. The town was hermetic. It was possible to know everyone. It was impossible to be anonymous. In that town at that time there was not one person who publicly identified as anything other than heterosexual. There was no one who identified as Aboriginal. There was one bloke who supposedly had one Korean parent, and he was the extent of our Asian population. The homogeneity was stultifying, and without the crude markers of race or sexuality it amplified more subtle differences between citizens. There was a dominant paradigm of masculinity, and I bought into it, sort of, from the sidelines. I learned to admire the courage of the footballer who backed into a marking contest or did not shirk a collision when sprinting toward a loose ball.

I know those places, my uncle said. Grew up in several of them myself. The veneration of the footy star. Some of them had no redeeming features whatsoever except for their lack of physical cowardice in a sporting context, but nevertheless they were local heroes.

There were other people displaying courage in that town, I said – the courage to express views outside the conservative and sometimes redneck norm. The courage of those few adults and students at my school who made a point of chatting to the kid with an intellectual disability, when no one else would give him any attention except

---

51 Carson McCullers: 'I must go home periodically to renew my sense of horror.' Quoted in Virginia Spencer Carr, *Understanding Carson McCullers*

52 'We look at the world once, in childhood./The rest is memory.' Louise Glück, 'Nostos'

through bullying. The courage of those who proselytized for their religion, however wrongheaded, and were persecuted for it. The courage of those who were not interested in football, and said so. But even though I saw this with my eyes, I did not compute it properly as courage at that time. After all, none of them was going to take a pack mark at centre-half-back.

28.

Have you asked yourself how Grim didn't die in the ring?

Yes, I said. Constantly.

Clearly he had unusual physical attributes, but he also endured physical abuse [53] unprecedented and unrepeated in that sport. Did Australian spectators hope to see him die in front of their eyes? Unlikely. But did that possibility add frisson? Of course. Part of boxing's enduring allure is that the stakes are so high. Combatants can die in any match.

I was fairly young when I read about Benny Paret being bludgeoned to death by Emile Griffith in their 1962 welterweight world title fight. I learned at that time that Paret had disrespected Griffith at the weigh-in, calling him a 'maricón,' and thus I learned that a disparaging reference to another man's sexuality provided an explanation for killing him.

A fine lesson for all Australian boys to internalize.

As you know, the story is complicated by the confirmation decades later that Griffith was bisexual. [54]

I don't think that complicates anything much at all. Have you seen the footage? Disturbing to think that it went out live-to-air.

---

53 'Joe Grim should be banned from ring,' *Pittsburgh Press*, 23 February 1904: 'Nothing could be more opposed to the spirit of true sport. A fair match and even chance for victory is the ideal that should govern all contests. To let a giant hammer a poorly conditioned youth (Grim) is to degenerate the ring into an abattoir. The kind of an audience that can cheer this spectacle would find equal delight at a pigsticking.'

54 Griffith once said, 'I kill a man and most people forgive me. However, I love a man and many say this makes me an evil person.' (Quoted in Donald McRae, *A Man's World: The Double Life of Emile Griffith*)

I was much older when I finally saw it. The act of watching Paret being bludgeoned into a coma from which he did not wake makes the viewer feel complicit, even decades later,[55] but detached from the dreadful outcome it is not an unusually ugly spectacle.

No, it is a fairly unexceptional fight that has been muddied by the attention of generations of writers and filmmakers. Watch footage of Griffith's explosive flurry at the end of the fight and compare it with Norman Mailer's hyperbolic report 'The Death of Benny Paret' for an object – abject – lesson in how history can be warped. After a competitive fight, Griffith began to dominate, then finished the contest with a series of hard rights delivered so quickly that the referee's hesitation to intervene was explicable if not justifiable. None of which is reflected in Mailer's twisted nonsense.

I agree. Griffith-Paret was not one of the hundreds of hideous one-sided bouts that make you question how anyone can watch combat sports in good conscience.[56] It was not like the brutalizing of Randall 'Tex' Cobb by Larry Holmes, which came just two weeks after Ray Mancini ended Kim Duk-koo's life in another boxing tragedy. The suffering was not prolonged like Vitali Klitschko dismantling Shannon Briggs. It was a sequence of rapid unanswered blows from Griffith to a well-matched challenger that lasted just under twenty seconds, and ended in tragedy.

When the combat-sport fan witnesses a one-sided beatdown, it exposes the uncomfortable extent to which we are voyeurs as well as spectators. Makes it much harder to hide from that dirty secret.

---

55 Or perhaps especially when it is viewed at this time remove, because watching the fight with the foreknowledge of Paret's fate changes this from a sporting experience and pushes the spectator toward – although not, I think, into – the shadow realm of snuff film.

56 '[Man] is the only creature that inflicts pain for sport, knowing it to be pain.' Mark Twain, *Autobiography Volume 2*

I know. Try watching the film of Ricardo Arona destroying Kazushi Sakuraba in a fight[57] that would not seem to end. Certainly, it was how I felt when Glover Teixeira smashed[58] Anthony Smith, a destruction so absolute and endless that Teixeira could be heard apologizing to Smith[59] as he wrestled him on the ground after knocking several teeth out of his mouth. It was a sickening spectacle, and I watched every minute.

It is not uncommon for people to die from single punches. Grim withstood hundreds of blows every fight. He was a one-off, the ultimate boxing outlier, but his metier was resilience rather than resistance. He absorbed and accepted.

Also, the pain he endured was a choice, and I think there is a difference between the pain you choose to endure and the pain you do not choose but must endure. Or is there? If you are choosing to endure pain, can that ever be a real choice? Must this willing acceptance by definition be impelled by something else so powerful that 'choice' is an illusion, the internal contradiction being that if you are rationally submitting to pain you are demonstrating your lack of rationality?

You might be thinking too hard. That can be painful, especially for those who have to spend time with you.

I'm not ignorant. My history is a digest of many types of pain. Mental pain, of course, which hurts most, but I have broken bones and snapped ligaments and endured frequent migraines. The most acute physical pain I have encountered was when I was eighteen and destroyed my knee in a play-wrestling manoeuvre that went wrong.

---

57   Pride MMA, 2005

58   UFC, 2020

59   Teixeira: Sorry, Anthony, part of the job.
       Smith: What?
       Teixeira: Sorry. Part of the job.
       Smith: It is what it is.

That has led to chronic aching in that knee ever since. Pain is familiar to me. And yet when I think of submitting myself, like Grim, to the caprices of another man's fists, I quail. The absence of control. The public spectacle. The not knowing. Perhaps my imagination is too strong and my empathy too well-developed, but I don't have the mental strength to endure that sort of physical abuse. Some people do. Grim, clearly, but certain other sports people also. [60]

Yes. And some soldiers. Some people in some religious settings. Perhaps others.

My closest experience of this is an extremely long way from Grim's experience, but it is all I have to measure with, to check how I might fare if faced with his challenges. When I was sixteen I competed in a district high schools open-age 400-metre race. It was on a proper running track in our regional centre. I had only ever run on grass before. I did not expect to do well. I was wearing clunky Dunlop KT-26 runners and work shorts. Everyone else in the race had swish running spikes and was wearing proper sports gear. But I had one huge advantage over my rivals from the bigger towns: it was a day of ferocious wind. The race went as I had anticipated, and I was coming last as we reached the final bend of the track. Entering the home straight meant running into the

---

60 Not just boxing. In a 22 September 2013 *Daily Telegraph* interview, George Piggins was asked to verify a famous story that in a rugby league brawl between South Sydney and Manly in 1973 he gouged Malcolm Reilly's right eye out of its socket before it slid back into place. Piggins said: 'I saw things that looked like tentacles on the back of my fingers as it was coming out. Malcolm had a big reputation as a tough bloke. He started the fight and it was me or him. We'd had a blue earlier in the match when he kicked me in the face and I put one on his chin. Then later on as he marked me to play the ball Malcolm struck his boot down my face and tore the bottom of my gums off my teeth. I butted him and threw him on to the ground and got on top of him. He went for my eyes and I gave back as good as I got. I don't drink but later on we had a lemonade and shook hands.'

comically strong wind, and it felt like colliding with a wall, but suddenly I realized that I had run through that wall and pushed to the lead. What the other runners did not know was that while they were honing their technique with athletics coaches, I was carrying fence posts around a farm. And while they were relaxing with girlfriends or boyfriends or going to the movies, the only way I could ease the jangling inside me was to go to the steepest hill in town and hammer out repeat sprints, up and down, up and down. The force of the wind made the race into a test of strength and willingness to endure pain. [61] As I threshed down the home straight I had only one competitor alongside. Who was prepared to hurt most, me or him? The pain in my lungs and my legs was difficult to endure. There were hundreds of people watching, from a dozen different towns. It was an opportunity to reveal myself as someone different to the person the mob had decided I was; and I was sixteen, an age at which many man-boys want to demonstrate, in front of peers and elders, their ability to shrug away pain. I could see the finish tape juddering in the gale. I had no air left, and the wind seemed to be blowing us backwards. I lost proper sensation in my legs, became uncertain where the bottom of each stride would be. I was in agony. The other runner was beside me, to my right, still no one else in my peripheral vision.

What happened?

---

61 Athletes generally nominate the 400 metre and the one-lap hurdles as the most painful events on the track because of the duration of anaerobic effort. Success in these events depends on foot speed, fitness, and pain forbearance. Each element is of roughly similar value. Thus, if the competitor who is fastest and fittest also has the capacity or willingness to endure the most pain, that competitor will always win. However, the fittest person may not win if they lack natural speed and the willingness to eat pain, and a pure pain artiste can triumph if they have reasonable fitness and speed. In the race that I am writing about, my guess is that I had the lowest foot speed, close to the highest fitness, and slid through on greater pain appetite on that particular day in those very specific conditions.

And then, with the line almost reached: I gave up. I was so close, but the pain won. I submitted and walked the last step or two over the line. Except that the runner on my right must have given up a moment before I did. I was the winner. District schools open champion. It qualified me to travel to the city to compete in the state championships, but I had seen the winning times for that age group in previous years and knew I would not get within cooee of anyone at that level, even in a typhoon. I had my one moment, ever, of sporting glory. And yet. I know, even if no one else does, that I gave in before the line. Broke. Surrendered to the pain. I also remember, although no one else would, that my physical reaction after the race was so intense that I had to withdraw from anchoring the 4 x 100 metre relay, and let my team down. I also know how shamefully proud I was of coming first in that regional race, a sin made sillier by the knowledge that on a still day I would never have won. But I didn't cry.

No, of course you didn't.

I have not experienced anything like that since, a public exhibition of my will, or lack of it. Or – unless – this is it. Could my unfulfilled writing career, replete with self-sabotage and a propensity for mock-heroic failure, be my own version of Grim's pain pantomime? Exercising all the talent I have in something I love, falling always short of success (deliberately, at some level?), refusing to stop writing, convincing myself that I am trying my best and the pain of mediocrity is all part of the deal? The perverse spectacle of constructing a life out of losing yet persevering, bewildering witnesses to our willingness to sacrifice dignity and our unwillingness to stop.

Sure. You can style the ongoing embarrassment of your unexceptional career as a glorious refusal to conform to audience dictates, performatively embodying the stubborn idealist who chooses to never write what others want to read.

Thus I am not an abject failure as a writer: no, I am triumphing in my own contest on my own terms. And it makes me about as happy as it made Grim, although less wealthy.

29.

Uncle Michael, maybe no blood relative but definitely terribly old, strained the dregs of sherry from the stained teacup and gestured for me to refill it. As soon as the task was complete, he continued:

There is a certain sound familiar to anyone who has been present during the castration or dehorning of cattle: a thick angry wallowing bellow. Whether you are beneath the steer doing the marking or at the bail end of the cattle crush with the guillotine dehorners or just standing alongside in nauseated witness, the sound is other-worldly; it seems to emanate from everywhere at once, oppressive and dismaying. Cracking open the door to the Ladies' Lounge, that was the sound and that was the way the sound behaved: as if all four walls simultaneously broadcast the same hyper-amplified groan-yell. Our arrival was of interest to no one. There was a puddle of spilled beer in the middle of the jarrah floor, threaded with red tendrils of blood. Two billiard cues were placed either side of the puddle, perhaps three feet apart. Air choked with pipe smoke thick as gruel, and fetid male humidity. Grim and I ordered beer and kept out of the way on one of the bench seats.

There were maybe twenty men in the room, some without boots, some without shirts, many bearded, almost all dishevelled. An exception was Dick Baddinton, who stood with his back to the bar, right foot raised onto the rail behind him, with a piece of quarto paper and a fountain pen. Next, he bawled, is another first round contest. Horrie Merkel and Dingo Flynn. Get into position, blokes.

Two of the bushmen put down their drinks and sidled to centre floor. One offered the other choice of side, and they shook hands, and then each got onto their hands and knees behind a billiard stick. Right you are, said Baddinton. Three, two, one, whooshka. On the last syllable of his final word the men exploded from their crouch, rocketing their heads toward each other until they collided with a sick crack. Then, immediately, that injured angry bellow of the marked, dehorned steer, stentorian, from one man or both and also the four walls, the sound so swirling and loud it was hard to determine. Come on, Horrie, someone said. You got him. All right then, Baddinton said, three – each resumed his starting position behind a cue – two, one, whooshka. Again the explosion forward, hands and knees down, nothing making contact except the top of their heads. Again the bellowing, clearly from both men now, laced with curse words. Just one more good one and he's gone, Dingo, someone said. Baddinton reloaded the count, three – back behind the billiard cues – two, one, but as he uttered whooshka one of the men pulled upright, raised his hand, and it was over. Dingo concedes, Horrie the winner, and through to round two, said Baddinton. Thanks, fellas. They shambled back to their drinks.

Grim sat with his legs crossed, nursing the beer in its chipped glass, stern focus on proceedings. I surveyed the room, eyes adjusting now to the fug. Every man had some sort of drink in his hand, beer or spirits. Many foreheads were maroon and puce, livid with battery, and it was difficult to guess which men were the winners and which the losers. There were vertical cuts, horizontal splits, stray gobbets of blood on cheeks and chests that the men had missed when wiping themselves down. Conversation was low and colloquial and apparently convivial.

This'll be the last first-round contest, hollered Baddinton. Bert Cooper and Yellerbeard. Into position, fellas. Derisory cheering that stopped almost as it started, and two men in their fifties approached the marks. Yellerbeard was clearly the bloke with a yellow beard, and twine around his dungarees. His opponent, presumably Cooper, wore tattered trousers under which could be glimpsed long underwear and a wooden leg. He removed his spectacles, tucked them into his coat pocket, and nimbly assumed the position. Yellerbeard flexed his neck left and right, opened and closed his jaw, and reluctantly dropped to the four-point stance. Right you are, said Baddinton. Three, two, one. And I have no reason to doubt that at that moment he said whooshka but I did not hear it. At that instant I made the mistake of glancing into the furthest corner of the room. In the murk there was a gargantuan hairless creature, naked and secured by a neck chain. The creature was covered in pink skin, grotesque gut dragging on the floor, tiny vicious eyes set deep in his porcine head. In his left fist he clutched a school shirt that he used to swipe at the sweat drizzling from his arse crack, at the drool spuming from his mouth, at his rheumy eyes. He saw me looking at him. The eyes bleeped with contempt. Without breaking my gaze he rubbed the shirt methodically around his distended corpus, then shovelled as much of it as he could inside his mouth.

By the time I looked away, the man with the yellow beard was lying on his side in the beer blood puddle and vocalizing his pain, and the pain of his ancestors, and the pain of any and all who catch themselves alive on this mystifying planet. Cooper retrieved his spectacles, paused to see if his adversary would like a hand up, then went looking for his drink. This is fascinating, Grim said. The calculation each one makes. The ideal situation is to get underneath your opponent so you can crack upward with the top of your skull into his face. However, if you duck down too early to look for the upward strike, a clever opponent might pause a split second and come over the top and strike down at you, their forehead to the back of your skull, which is the most vulnerable part. So competitors who don't want to take a risk meet square on, presenting the top of the skull. This protects the bones of the face and the softer areas at the back of the head. You can certainly win that way, but it will take more blows, and most men won't stay that journey. It's a nice sporting conundrum. I just wish the standard of participants was higher. The judgment would have been pompous coming from a different mouth, but Grim could not be stopped by Jack Johnson, Philadelphia Jack O'Brien, or the original Joe Walcott. Not one of them got the better of his skull.

Mind if I sit with you. It was Cooper, the winning man, glass in hand, a red welt above his left eye. Yes, of course, I said. Bert Cooper, he said. Congratulations, I said. What is that you're drinking? McWilliams sherry, he said. Royal Reserve, I said. You know it, he said. I need to sit when I can. The leg, you know. It's a fine-looking leg, I said. I machined it myself, he said, put a piece of karri on the lathe and kept trimming until it fit snug. Came up nicely, didn't it. You're not from around here, he said. No, I said, we – we're travelling. Travelling, he said. You're likely Perth-bound. I think that's the plan, I said.

Baddinton called up the second-round participants, men who had won their opening bouts. Cy Rutter and Archibald Jenkins took their places, waited for the count, smashed their heads together like a locomotive coupling with a caboose, again the deep-chested howling, unhappy angst amplified into a dirty gush of sound. The next pairing was Billabong Koufax and Edward Coffin. Koufax dipped low and drove upward, the tactic Grim identified, and there was a sound like an oar smacking water, and Coffin staggered to his feet, reeled, fell against the bar. Baddinton started the next count, the stricken Coffin could not make it to his mark in time, Koufax was the winner. When Coffin removed his hand from his face, we could see the damage: the upwards head-butt had gashed his eye socket so deeply it created an extra opening through which the eyeball leered, giving him the garish appearance of a man with three eyes. There was a gentle tide of warm acclamation when the assembled company witnessed the facial transfiguration.

The next pair was summonsed, more grunting and rupturing and writhing. Who do you challenge next, I said to Cooper. Not entirely sure, he said. It doesn't really matter. I did not know how to ask about the creature in the corner but he saw me slant my gaze that way; I could not stand to look there and I could not look away: the paradox of horrified transfixion. Ah yes, he said. Because you are new here you probably don't know the rules. Whichever man wins the head-butt tournament gets to drink at the pub free for a week. Then there is the additional challenge, which not many men take up. The winner also has the right to take on Pig Thug. Victory in that contest means he drinks at the pub free for the rest of his life.

Who is Pig Thug, I asked, although the answer was gleamingly obvious. Pig Thug is the hotel mascot, Cooper said. They got him from some little town over east, dug him up out of the deep past, and now they keep him chained in the shed during the day and in the front bar at night. They used to have a problem with people breaking in looking for liquor or money, but since they acquired Pig Thug the burglaries have stopped. He doesn't cost much to keep. They let him drink from the slops tray, and he eats whatever tucker is placed in front of him – table scraps, stock feed, old meat, it makes no difference.

Has he ever been beaten at head-butting, I said, although again the question seemed redundant. Of course not, said Cooper. Look at him. There have only been three or four men stupid enough to try their luck, and two ended their efforts at the undertaker's premises. The sawbones told us the average thickness of the human male skull is one-quarter of an inch – although it varies. Frontal bone averages one-quarter-inch thickness, temporal three-twentieths of an inch, central frontal bone eight-twenty-fifths, and parietal eleven-fiftieths. The occipital bone, well where do we start – let's just say it averages about two-fifths of an inch thickness, but of course over the cruciform eminence it is much more, on other planes far less. Many's the night I've sat here with the doc and he has talked us through the science. The cortical thickness of the skull changes dramatically with age in females but not males, which is a very lucky bloody thing indeed.

But Pig Thug's skull is calculated at three or four inches thick right around. You'll notice that he has a comparatively small noggin; trust me when I say that it is almost pure bone.

Grim did not appear to be paying attention to us. He was still intent on each contest, grunting as the action commenced, moving his body fractionally forward or back in jerky kinesthetic mimicry. Baddinton called for the final second-round pair, Horrie Merkel to face Bert Cooper. I wished Cooper well, and he sighed, and clumped across to the mark without looking back, secreted his specs in his jacket pocket, lowered himself on three limbs while sliding the base of his finely turned wooden leg backwards, and waited in place on knees and knuckles. On whooshka the two grizzled contestants lurched forward, parietal bones meeting so flush that their respective sagittal sutures might have knitted together. Enormous groans, oaths, vigorous rubbing of horned hands through thinning hair. Baddinton, relentless, commenced the count again: then whooshka, but, and for whatever reason, Cooper lifted his face, his sad gaze finding my own, like a soon-drowned man taking a last glimpse about him, and at that instant Merkel's head hurtled through like a cannonball. It caught Cooper across the left side of his face. The dapper man collapsed like a sack emptied of potatoes, and the bout was clearly over. I hurried to Cooper's prone form, realized that no one else was interested in assisting, and did not need medical training to understand that he was badly hurt. His left cheekbone was depressed, his nose askew with a glimpse of bone through a gash just below the bridge, and his left eye was swollen closed. I said to the barman, This man needs a doctor, right now. He looked lazily at Cooper on the floor and said, Give him a chance to come good, I know Bert, he'll be right as rain. Another sherry or two, sleep it off, and he'll be cherry ripe in a couple of days. I said, His cheekbone is obviously fractured, his nose is broken, and the blood inside the eye makes me think the orbital bone is smashed, too. Yeah, said the barman, could be. Bert, you want another Royal Reserve, cobber? Mate, he said to me, just help him over to the bench, will ya. Need to clear the area for the semis. Sure enough, Baddinton lifted his swelling voice above the hubbub and announced the penultimate contests.

Cooper released a ceaseless string of blood and sputum as I lugged him to the bench seat. He's real crook, I said to Grim. Bloke needs a doctor. Grim turned his head and frowned at Cooper's mangled countenance. He'll be sore for a few days, Grim said. Get him a drink. I ordered a sherry at the bar. The barman held his ham hand out for payment. I said, Surely this is on the house – the bloke's half-dead. The barman said, If Bert can't pay for his drink that's no problem. Just means you'll have to buy it for him. I stood my ground for about a second, then paid, and walked back lugging the drink and my humiliation.

I had sickened of the spectacle. Wanted to be somewhere else. Wanted not to recall that when Cooper looked at me in that instant, I saw in his eyes that he was seeing something in mine. And then the carnage came.

Baddinton sooled the semifinalists into action. Koufax and Merkel won those contests, and were matched for the grand reckoning, but Merkel was staggering like a man walking on loose marbles, and then he erupted with a parabolic arc of vomit that was discharged near the bar and landed on the jarrah floorboards near the door, and then he took four unsteady steps forward and collapsed chin first. Someone ambled across and checked his pulse. Still alive, he said, returning to the bar. Maybe that was Cooper's mate, the sawbones.

Baddinton was not happy. This is the single worst thing about head-butting, he said. You wait all day for the defining contest and then it is thrown away with complete disregard. He seemed to blame Horrie Merkel for succumbing to coma. Well youse all know the rules, Baddinton said, voice brittle with frustration. Can't have a champion without a championship bout. One of you bastards is gonna have to step up. Who's on for it? Come on, you bludgers, just one go-round against a bloke who's already sick from three hard contests, and you could get a free week on the piss and the right to challenge Pig Thug. You're two wins away from drinks for the rest of your days, all on the house. Baddinton started moving around the room, gripping this or that man by the upper bicep and urging them to step up. No volunteers. He reached our bench, ignoring the stricken form of Cooper rocking himself and clutching at his shattered face. How about you, he started to say to me and then said, No, never mind. I said, What do you mean never mind? He glanced at me, flat, as if to say surely you're aware of what I'm looking at,[62] and I blushed and said, Yes, never mind.

He looked instead at Grim. What about you, cobber? Why doncha give it a burl. Drink free for a week if you win. That's not much use to me, said Grim. We are moving on tomorrow. What about five pounds if I win, and fifty if I defeat that creature in the corner? Baddinton stared at him hard. You are kidding yourself, mate, he said. No cash prizes. And you wouldn't last a minute with Pig Thug, anyway. I'd enjoy trying, said Grim. Easy words to say, mate, said Baddinton. What are you, anyway – some sort of dago? We don't get many dagos out this way. Dago rock chopper, I'm thinking, a breed famous for their yellow bellies. You want to prove different, get down there and take on Koufax for the honour and glory. Grim pressed his lips outward. Or are you another dago cur, said Baddinton, gonna run like a schoolgirl with wet knickers. Eh. Coward dago, I reckon.

Five pounds the win, fifty if I beat that blob, said Grim. Pig Thug indicated his enthusiasm, yanking my school shirt from his mouth and waving it around his head. Baddinton pressed the

---

62 In terms of Melville's *White-Jacket*, always a Rose-Water, never a May-Day.

needle deeper. Coward dago, like all dagos, only happy sucking on mama's titties. Get down there and show otherwise, or we'll know what you are, a greasy Papist pantywaist. More words like that. Grim sat unmoved, unbowed.

Baddinton, bereft, cursed and flapped his hands in Grim's face, and moved off to hassle someone else. Grim may have smiled, almost, and padded over to the murkiest corner to take a closer look at Pig Thug. [63] The creature spat at his visitor; the green splodge hit Grim's trousers but he made no attempt to clean it off. He peered at the pink hairless nightmare like a last-chance bettor appraising a horse in the mounting yard, then nodded his head to himself, and raised his chin at me, and we left the hotel, and stricken Cooper and the other men in critical condition or merely bruised and contused and concussed, and did not see the concluding contest or contests, and spent a quiet night preparing for departure further west the next morning.

---

63 'Man, in his highest and noblest capacities, is wholly nature and embodies its uncanny dual character. Those of his abilities which are terrifying and considered inhuman may even be the fertile soil out of which alone all humanity can grow in impulse, deed, and work.' Friedrich Nietzsche, *Homer's Contest*

30.

Hilary Mantel's 'Ten Rules for Writing Fiction,' number 3, in part:

Don't write for a perceived audience or market. It may well have vanished by the time your book's ready.

Well yes, it might. But readers of the Norguna Ladies' Lounge scene might vanish a lot more swiftly.

31.

Roland Barthes?

I know very close to nothing about him except that he died from injuries associated with being struck by a laundry van.

Yes, cleaned him right up. I know very little also, but you will see there by your feet Barthes's book *Mythologies* cracked open to 'The World of Wrestling,' and it was more decipherable than I had gloomily anticipated. Barthes's critique is useful for reminding me of what Grim was, and what he was not. He said that in professional wrestling, as in the theatre, 'what is expected is the intelligible representation of moral situations which are usually private'; Grim's work also only made sense as a public display. If he had pursued his pain art privately it would have been something else altogether. When Barthes refers to an 'Exhibition of Suffering … (that) presents man's suffering with all the amplification of tragic masks,' it evokes the simplicity of Grim's similar project.

The face that cunningly conceals the mask beneath.

That's almost profound. As for Barthes, he is not infallible: his assertion that 'the spectator does not wish for the actual suffering of the contestant; he only enjoys the perfection of an iconography' miscalculates the depravity of the human soul and misreads the emotions of wrestling (and boxing) fans. His belief that 'wrestling is the only sport which gives such an externalized image of torture' suggests he was not au fait with Grim's oeuvre, did not remember Jack Dempsey against Jess Willard, and did not countenance Luis Resto against Billy Collins Jr., let alone your friend Glover Teixeira traducing Anthony Smith. More helpfully, he links the display in the ring to 'ancient myths of public Suffering and Humiliation: the cross and the pillory.'

Grim and his pain pantomime.

Ultimately the thing he finds in wrestling, however, is a world set to rights, [64] something at complete cross-purposes to the sense-bending anathema of Grim: 'the euphoria of men raised for a while above the constitutive ambiguity of everyday situations and placed before the panoramic view of a univocal Nature, in which signs at last correspond to causes, without obstacle, without evasion, without contradiction.' Against this we stand Joe Grim, a man from the fun-fair sideshow tradition, a man [65] who reminds us of where the bounds of the normal are drawn and stands conspicuously and spectacularly outside that compass. Without obstacle, without evasion, without contradiction.

---

64   'Pro wrestling has long been a land of expansiveness, a playground for literally outsize men to act out metaphorically outsize tropes and storylines for the teleological gratification of the masses.' David Shoemaker, *The Squared Circle: Life, Death and Professional Wrestling*

65   '[B]oxers have frequently displayed themselves, inside the ring and out, as characters in the literary sense of the word. Extravagant fictions without a structure to contain them.' Joyce Carol Oates, *On Boxing*

32.

You haven't offered me any of that delicious sherry, I said.

Are you a grown-up? I figured you would be capable of attending to your own needs.

I don't think that is a sure bet, I said.

He gazed out across the eastern bank. Periodicals and annual reports and first editions and chapbooks. I reached with my foot and gave the pile a gentle push. It did not move. Perhaps there would be no landslide and I would live another day.

These old memories of Grim, I said, do they feel nearer to you than things that have happened more recently? (Isn't this something old people always say? Perhaps I was just trying to distract him from becoming completely blotto.)

I don't know, he said, but one thing I do know is that time is elastic, and the people worst at understanding that are whitefella adults: people like me. We know sometimes time runs fast and sometimes it runs slow, seem to be able to cope with that, but there are also vertical slices through time where other commonalities are in place and the chronology ceases to be important, the fusion of past and present, or even the complete moving on from the spurious notion of 'past' – I'm sure there are holes in time's fabric where a little light can peek through, but you need to know how to see it.

He took a swig from his cup, then a swig from the open mouth of the flagon, then another swig from the cup. I've got bored, he said. Bored of words. Look at this place! Sitting here in the valley of the mountains of words, which is all I've accumulated in a lifetime, that and a few suspect memories. So tired of words! What do you think, a million words in here? A million times a million? And that's how I've spent my allotted days. I should have been painting watercolours of quetzals and cassowaries, should have taught children how to repair bicycles, should have made love with at least one person from every country in the world, should have started a laughter farm. Built a hut in a forest and slept the clock around on a mattress woven from cottonwool and psithurism. But no, I chose words. Goddamn words. I wish there was any other way[66] to get to the end of this too-long Grim tale. Bored, bored, bored! But you've come this far. I'll push on.

---

66 'As soon as we start putting our thoughts into words and sentences everything gets distorted, language is just no damn good – I use it because I have to, but I don't put any trust in it. We never understand each other.' Marcel Duchamp, quoted in Enrique Vile-Matas's *Bartleby & Co.*

33.

Continuing the bibliotherapy, he said.

After attending his first ever fight, between William Neate and Thomas 'Gas-man' Hickman at Hungerford, Berkshire, on 11 December 1821, William Hazlitt wrote: 'I never saw anything more terrific than his aspect just before he fell. All traces of life, of natural expression, were gone from him. His face was like a human skull, a death's head, spouting blood. The eyes were filled with blood, the nose streamed with blood, the mouth gaped blood. He was not like an actual man, but like a preternatural, spectral appearance, or like one of the figures in Dante's *Inferno*. Yet he fought on after this for several rounds, still striking the first desperate blow, and Neate standing on the defensive, and using the same cautious guard to the last, as if he had still all his work to do; and it was not till the Gas-man was so stunned in the seventeenth or eighteenth round that his senses forsook him, and he could not come to time, that the battle was declared over. Ye who despise the FANCY, do something to show as much pluck, or as much self-possession as this, before you assume a superiority which you have never given a single proof of by any one action in the whole course of your lives!'[67]

In his 200 CE treatise *Spectacles*, Berber theologian Quintus Septimius Florens Tertullianus condemned fight sports, arguing that it disfigured the divinely designed human form. In 500 CE the Ostrogoth king and ruler of Italy Theodoric the Great banned boxing because he believed that disfiguring a face through punching was an insult to God. In between those times, Roman emperor Theodosius I and church leaders Saint Jerome and Saint Augustine argued for the banning of fight sports due to connections to paganism. In 2017

---

67   Essay, 'The Fight'

CE Conor McGregor fought Floyd Mayweather Jr. in a Las Vegas event that generated in excess of US$400,000,000.

34.

My uncle was stretched sideways across the carpet, head on the second volume of the *Shorter Oxford* (Marl-Z and Addenda), feet on a short stack of back issues of *The Fist*. He cradled the sherry flagon like a faithful cat.

I have noticed, I said, that there are no women in your stories.

You want me to invent something? Like me to rewrite things to retrofit some female presence that never existed?

But there must have been women, I persisted.

Not in the ring.

Was Grim gay?

What a peculiar conclusion. I think he had a wife[68] in

---

68 Grim married Carrie 'Carolina' Sesso in 1902. (Note: This date is from a June 1971 *Sports Illustrated* story notable for its inaccuracies.) She was born 31 August 1884 in Italy and died 22 September 1971 in Philadelphia. There is scant information about her, although she is referred to in passing in the *Saint Paul Globe*, 12 February 1905: Grim, arguing that he should be excused from jury duty, is quoted as saying, 'Mean shame ... I needa da mon. Wife, she needa da mon.' They are buried together in Holy Cross Cemetery, Delaware County, in Pennsylvania. It appears that they had one child, Umberto Giannone, born and died 1903. Grim had thirteen recorded fights in 1903, including bouts with some of his highest-credentialed opponents – Joe Gans, Peter Maher, Bob Fitzsimmons, Philadelphia Jack O'Brien, and Joe Walcott. What sort of emotional pain was he enduring while absorbing punishment from these extraordinary hitters? Was it a relief to be in the ring, back with the familiarity of physical pain rather than the agonies of the heart? When he was in Australia in 1908–09, did he correspond with his wife? Did he send money home? They lived for some years in a narrow three-storey terrace at 747 Clymer Street in Philadelphia. What went on within those walls? Is anything ever more profoundly mysterious than other people's relationships?

Philadelphia, but he never spoke about her. As for his time in Australia – there are stronger motivations than sex.

Are there? Isn't sex in the centre of everything?

Your imagination is sorely limited. Or you are much younger than you look. But you want a woman in my story, so I will provide a woman. That's all I'm here to do, serve your whims. Call her … Dora. She lives in the pinprick Western Australian town of Billinup. We will give her the face of the young Concha Michel. [69] She has some of the verve of Isadora Duncan [70] as well as her interest in the particularities of human movement. Humorous rather than funny; wry and light and smart and twinkling. Does this make you happy? Salve some misguided fears about what equity should look like?

Sure, I said.

---

69   As per the famous photo, seemingly uncredited, in which Concha Michel looks fearless-eyed into the camera, body at a three-quarter tilt. Her dark straight hair is cut short and has a centre part that aligns with her nose and the indent in her chin: part owl, part swan. Dora's form and her dress will be borrowed from the Tina Modotti photo of Michel playing a twelve-string guitar in a dusty compound, watched by four older Mexican men in serapes and large-brimmed hats.

70   Thinking here of the Isadora Duncan, who wrote in *The Philosopher's Stone of Dancing*: 'Imagine then a dancer who, after long study, prayer and inspiration, has attained such a degree of understanding that his body is simply the luminous manifestation of his soul; whose body dances in accordance with a music heard inwardly, in an expression of something out of another, profounder world. This is the truly creative dancer; natural but not imitative, speaking in movement out of himself and out of something greater than all selves.' (What Isadora might have made of Benny Leonard or Sugar Ray Robinson or Willie Pep.)

35.

There was a guest house in Billinup where we could hole up for a week or so. Grim did not want to get to Perth too early. Too expensive, he said. His fight against Bob Fraser was slated for the Theatre Royal, twenty rounds. R. G. Salter, the promoter, was billing Fraser as The Hardest Hitter in Australia, and Twice Conqueror of Bill Lang, with Grim, of course, listed as The Iron Man and the event averred to be The Contest of the Decade. It was the old irresistible force/immovable object pitch, easy for even the slowest peon to latch onto. Lang – William Lanfranchi – was now the Australian and Commonwealth heavyweight champ and one of the country's greatest fighters, but Fraser met him when he was a stripling, in Lang's second and eighth bouts, and claimed victories via disqualification and then points. Fraser was no mug, with sixteen wins, ten losses, one draw, ten of the wins by knockout. He had two cracks at the Victorian middleweight title and one at the welterweight belt and lost all three, and his career and skills were in decline. Of course, you don't put that on a promotional poster.

As we waited in the guest house front room for the woman who owned the place to do some protracted business with a pencil and a ruler and a dusty notebook, I flipped through a pile of newspapers. You have papers from all over, I said. Every state in the colony, Britain, America, she said. The prospectors carry them along as a distraction on the steamship trip across and then don't want to carry them any further when they are striking out to the diggings. I peeled open a grimy copy of the *Washington Times*, dated 25 July 1905. Have a look at this, I said to Grim.

MARVELOUS ITALIAN STOOD OFF JOHNSON FOR SIX ROUNDS – SAVED BY BELL IN LAST SESSION – HOLDS THE RECORD

By TAD [71]

The bell clanged last night at the National Athletic club in the sixth round amid the wildest excitement ever seen at a fight.

Joe Grim, the sturdy Italian who has faced the greatest men in the world without being counted out, had met Jack Johnson, and it looked as though he had met his Waterloo. He was down for the tenth time in that round, and lay there writhing in pain, hundreds around the ring hatless and coatless, yelling like mad, his seconds running around throwing water and begging him to try and get up, and the referee counting eight, just as the bell sounded, and saved Grim from what looked to be certain defeat. He stayed the limit with the giant black man, but every speck of gameness was brought to play to land him on his feet.

It was a sight that one seldom sees, and one that will linger long in the memory of the people. Grim had fought gamely for five rounds. He took terrible lefts on the body, nose and mouth without flinching, and went to his corner round after round looking more like a hamburger steak than a human being. He came up smiling for the sixth, and as he shook hands with his powerful opponent said: 'Joe Grim is still here and you can't put him out.'

Big Johnson, looming up like a mountain of ebony, smiled, but in back of that smile was a desire to get action out of the Italian wonder. As they squared off the big black giant rushed

---

71   TAD was Thomas Aloysius Dorgan, who, apart from being a star boxing writer and a gifted cartoonist, was a savant at inventing widely adopted slang terms. You pay unknowing tribute to him when you use the term 'lounge lizard,' or 'hard-boiled,' or 'for crying out loud,' or 'the cat's pyjamas,' or say, 'Yes, we have no bananas.' When he was thirteen, three of his fingers were severed in a factory machine. At the other end of his life he was sick for a long time. Between times he was brilliant. He died at fifty-two.

and drove a crushing right on Grim's jaw. Joe's head rolled back, he went down slowly, and then rolled over on his back. The crowd howled and howled as Referee McGuigan counted, but Grim gamely arose, only to be crushed again. Nine different times he had gone to the floor in that round from the pile-driving smashes of the giant negro, and as he rolled over from the last one every man in the house thought that his time had come. Grim had been beaten almost to a pulp in this round, and as he stopped the last uppercut on the jaw and rolled over on his back without the slightest sign of life, it did really look as though he was out for good.

He fell over on his back, his head almost out of the ring, and there he lay, the referee getting closer to the fatal 'ten' and the excitement getting wilder and wilder, just as the gong came to his rescue.

Four seconds carried the disabled fighter to his corner, where he was worked on until he came to and then he got up smiling, looked for Johnson, and shook hands with him. Johnson's eyes were sticking out and he was as rattled as any man in the house, seeing how near he had come to putting the Italian down for the limit. Even as he left the ring his legs were wobbly and he was still dazed from the terrible punishment. If there is a man in the world who can put the brave Italian out, he is yet to be seen.

That's okay, Grim said.

Strange life, this one. Your head must spin, tangling with the giant Johnson on that side of the world, now preparing for Bob Fraser over here, but at least Fraser will provide a quiet night, I said.

There is no quiet night, he said. I may play the *bouffon*, but this is all of my being.

After we checked into our room, he dispatched me to the Billinup store with a shopping list. The shop was well-stocked and cheerful and I tossed Grim's shopping list onto the counter. The storeman bent close to the scrap of paper, picked it up, then held it in front of his eyes, raising and lowering his spectacles. I can't make this out, he said to me.

Six eggs
One hair comb
One gallon fresh bull piss

He wants six eggs, one hair comb, and one gallon of fresh bull piss, I said. Oh, I did read it right, the storeman said. It can be difficult to read these things when someone has an accent, I said. Well, he said, I can help you with the googs and the bug rake. But pretty sure we don't have any bull piss in stock just now, fresh or otherwise. I guess I am not surprised, I said. Do you have any idea where I can source some bull piss? So it has to be bull, not cow, and not some other male beast like a boar or a ram, he said. I believe so but I will double-check, I said. No, not really a clue, he said; sadly, I thought. I paid for the other goods and took them to Grim and asked him to clarify re the piss. Did it have to be bull, did it have to be a full gallon et cetera. I don't understand what the problem is, he said. Most general stores don't keep a lot of animal urine on hand, I said. And most people think sourcing piss from a bull is potentially dicey work. I see, he said. Well, ask around. I have used heifer piss before, but it's not much good. Maybe we could experiment with other creatures, I said; in fact if you'd thought of it back in the desert we could have asked the cretinous goat to help out, although I don't actually recall ever seeing the goat micturate. Well, it was very dry out there, Grim said.

I must have been developing plenty of fellow feeling for my travel companion because I borrowed a large metal pail from the woman who ran the guest house and obtained directions to the nearest dairy. I talked to the cocky, who agreed that obtaining urine from his one intact bull was a potentially fatal endeavour. Instead we made a collection from the milking cattle, three steers he had fattening for sale (I watched in astonishment as he held their back legs in the crook of one arm to stop them kicking), and even some poddy calves. I clanked and slopped the bucket of hot mixed piss back to our lodgings and Grim seemed well pleased.[72] He lowered his face into the liquid, kept it there while he held his breath for thirty seconds, came up for air, then repeated the effort. A dozen times over. He used the sleeve of his shirt to wipe his mouth clean but did not move a muscle to dab the piss off the rest of his face, the perimeter of his hairline et cetera. When it dripped off his sloping brow and into his eyes he merely blinked. Then he placed both hands inside the bucket and sat contentedly for perhaps fifteen minutes. He explained that this was the best way to inure his skin to the dangers of cuts and splitting. I am professional, he said, and a professional prepares properly. When we turned in later that evening, he lay on his side of the cot, me on mine, and my struggle for elusive slumber was not helped any by the acrid aroma of bovine urine. Grim snored, content, free of worry.

The following day he retrieved the pail and reprised the submersion treatment, then tipped the stinking liquid out into the garden. He told me that he felt more sure than ever that it was really only efficacious if the piss was fresh; I promised to try to get some more. He wandered outside to a blackbutt tree in the corner of the yard, removed his shirt, rotated his arms vigorously, then started punching the tree trunk. Dull, thudding straight punches, monotonous and identical. Bomm, bomm, bomm. I had seen many boxers train, but never a man without gloves striking an unrelenting object like this. He explained that it was a technique he had learned to try to strengthen his fists. Scientists said that repeated blows made bone

---

72 Jack Dempsey preferred to soak his face and hands in horse urine. See Roger Kahn, *A Flame of Pure Fire*.

denser and more durable. I said that scientists said the bumps on the back of his skull indicated a tendency toward sexual deviance. He said that the biggest threat to his earning capacity was the tendency of his small finger bones and knuckles to shatter, and on this he trusted the scientists, and also he had been examined by some of the world's best phrenologists already and they came to no such conclusion. He wished he had been born with large mitts because they spread the force of the punch across a bigger area, but God was not kind with his fist size, handing him hands with bones that snapped like twigs, so all he could do was try to toughen them through repeated trauma prior to fight dates. Facial skin less prone to cuts, hands less prone to cracking – the rest, then, was up to his hard skull and his wily distraction techniques and his brute willingness to endure body assaults.

I left him to his routine. He stopped periodically to balance on his head and swivel his body around that fulcrum, strengthening and making more supple the stalk his famous head perched upon. Then back to the metronomic hammering.

I found a doorway in which to perch and absorb some yellow sunlight. After a time I noticed that we were not alone. Grim had another observer. She sat on a low stone wall close to the kitchen at the rear of the guest house with a pad of paper and was watching Grim and then making marks on the page.

She was: entrancing; I felt there may have been a field of shimmering green electricity around her.

I felt like there was something caught in my throat. I felt dislocated. I felt that there was green electricity inside me. I thought the air buzzed. I thought I was no longer in the yard. I thought I had only ever been in the yard. This was something very strange; I felt unprepared; something too much, simultaneously all that I wanted and a cathedral I was not ready to enter. Do these words make no sense? I am trying to convey: it was a tiny rupture in the orderly sequence of life; I might wish, I *did* wish, to once, some time, see a woman whose presence would knock my head sideways, but it made my life feel infinitely less simple inside that instant, and I wished at one level at least that this was not happening, because. Because: everything. It is a strange thing to be a man. A young man. There are forces over which you have no governance, and it makes your head swim. Have I said enough? Do you remember, or imagine, that moment of opening your eyes and seeing someone impossibly unbearably entrancing? It happens from time to time but only when you are a certain age.

She was small and neatly built, simply dressed in a shift that came just below her knees with sleeves stopping above the elbow, a dress with no frills or adornment. When she stood and changed her vantage point, I saw that she moved with loping long steps, a languid easiness in her body. Her face was alert, intelligent, curious, knowing. I wondered if she was from somewhere else: her dark hair was straight and cut close to the head, a fashion I had not observed before. The crown was adorned with a single straight part, as a man might divide his hair – a part that formed a pale line that led, when followed downward, to the contiguous line of her pretty nose, and lower to the philtrum, and then the unexpected softness of a smudged dimple in the centre of her chin: all aligned. But her eyes: the gaze, unafraid, evaluating. Just as she stared at Grim, so I stared at her. And stared at her. And in that rapture, the rapture occurring within the rupture in the normal progress of time, it was at once one and zero, one and one million: all things were overlaid, simultaneity, congruity and incongruity, I am losing my words and my sense again. I know now that this seems foolish, a tank-load of sentiment emptied into a pond of self-delusion, but in that moment I believed that I was merged with her, a synthesis requiring just an eye blink, and so imperative was it that I understand her thoughts, that I was then seeing through her eyes, thinking with and through in her, a new world, contrived by proxy through the gaze of the only woman to have ever the only woman I had the only woman. Inside her skin; peering out through her peering out.

The young male brain is a bizarre country and I would not advise visiting, not ever.

36.

I have sailed many seas and seen many sights but nothing previous have I seen to prepare me for this. In the yard at the back of my guest house, a half-naked man punching repeatedly at a tree. There is nothing significant about his size or shape – a man of average height and unspectacular build – but a fierce animal energy fizzes from him. Transfixing. Periodically he pauses from pounding with his fists, flips upside down, and supports all of his weight on his head, while jerking his arms and legs back and forth. (I have not really sailed any seas, nor seen many sights. But I have never seen this in Billinup.)

When he is finished I sidle across, too curious to be off-put by embarrassment at seeming forward. You are new here, I say.

Uh.

You are from …

America. Italy.

How long have you been in Australia?

Seven months. This is a very big country.

W.A. is the largest portion, as well. I'm Dora. Dora Harwood.

Joe Grim.

So your original name must be Giuseppe?

No. Saverio. In America everyone think dagos are called Joe.

You say dago?

They say dago.

They say dago. Doesn't mean you have to say dago, surely?

Yeah.

I am fascinated by your calisthenics.

It's something I do.

I have never seen anyone punch a tree, and I have never seen anyone contort so vigorously while perched on their head.

It strengthens the hands, strengthens the neck.

I was very bold. I made some diagrams of what you were doing. I hope you don't mind. I have a lot of spare time here in Billinup and my grand scheme is to outline a taxonomy of human movement.

I have no idea what that means.

I am just at the beginning, thinking mainly at present about the pelvic girdle.

Okay.

It is this theory I am formulating. I think possibly all movement is predicated on what happens from that middle area, from the obturator foramen working out. The quality of activity around there, through the whole acetabulum and from the iliac crest to the ischial tuberosity, that is the source, I am theorizing, of all balance and power and generation of movement – and thus stage one for the taxonomy. What do you think of that?

You are what – twenty?

Nineteen.

You live here?

I am the teacher at Billinup school. I grew up in Albany, and I did not want to keep being in Albany. I have my own ideas, and young women with ideas are not much welcome anywhere, but especially not in the towns in which they have grown up. So I have come to Billinup as this opinionated outsider. I don't mind. I like teaching the children, and there is plenty of space to walk and time to think.

Where do you walk?

Are you done with your exercise regime? There is a string of billabongs I like to walk around. No one strolls for pleasure in Billinup, so it is pleasingly lonesome there. I can take you, if you wish.

It doesn't bother you to go off walking with a strange man?

I have known stranger.

You know I'm a fighting man? For money?

I have read very little of Mister Conan Doyle, but I guessed that a man with a face full of scar tissue and a nose no more solid than a wedge of tripe might be in the fisticuffs business. No, it doesn't bother me.

When I fight I watch the other man's hips.

You do? I am already three parts convinced that the most crucial point of all is the superior pubic ramus. If a dancer, or an athlete – or a boxer – was to think themselves into that part of their anatomy, to lock the ramus into the required pattern of movement and allow everything else to follow, like eyes following a match flame swung around in a darkened room, then that might be the secret to effortless, purposeful movement. As I say, I have had plenty of time to ponder! That is what my taxonomy is trying to capture, analyze, and enunciate so anyone might replicate the movements of the planet's finest movers. I don't want much! That's the schoolroom over there. Fifteen students on a good day, aged four to fourteen.

Mmh.

And there is the last house. Now we're officially out of town, and you can see the start of the chain of billabongs over here.

I fought a wrestler once. They said he had the ability to turn around inside his own skin. Whose cattle are those?

That's Methuselah's milking shed. I'm not certain of his real name. Long white beard.

No bulls?

I doubt it. It's just a milking herd.

I need some fresh bull piss.

Dare I ask?

It toughens and softens the skin, all at the one time.

I knew a man back in Albany who wore a lot of cologne. The men in Albany said there were things a girl should know about men who wore cologne. But I don't recall hearing anything about fellows splashing themselves in bull urine.

If I don't fight, I don't eat. If my skin splits, the doctors won't let me fight. My life is stupid, really.

Oh no, Mr. Grim! It might be absurd, but it is not stupid.

Mmh.

This billabong chain runs along an ancient riverbed. This was mostly virgin country, then the Yilgarn goldfields opened up and the roads pushed through. The locals tell me that the billabongs are spring-fed. They are proud of them – about the only thing anyone is proud of around here. Did you hear that Doodlakine down the road has put its name up to be capital of Australia?[73]

As good a place as any.

I am thinking, Mr. Grim …

Joe.

Mr. Joe Grim, perhaps you would not be averse to helping me with my studies. There is so much about human movement I long to understand, and doubtless I could learn from watching you.

Yes.

Well, I don't know if you are prudish about this sort of thing, but I would love to observe your form as you go through your fighting movements. To try to find the wellspring of your mechanical activity.

Yes?

We are perfectly alone.

Stripped?

Yes, please.

Si.

I am not afraid of the male form. Well – gracious. Yes, as I please. I'm very much obliged to you. This will be – perfect. Now can you show me your fighting stance? Okay, just like so? And do you stay still, or do you rock, or – Oh yes, I see. You don't mind me observing you so closely?

---

73   Margaret Grose, 'A Forgotten Capital,' *Australian Planner*

Okay.

Now move backwards for me, as if a fighter was advancing toward you. Uh. And move forwards, as if you were the aggressor. I see. And turn to your right, as if following a man that way. And back to the left. Oh, really. This is most interesting. And again to your right. And left. And moving backwards again, and then forwards. This is wonderful. Are you okay if I place my hands just here, to feel the rotation through your hips?

That's fine.

Fine. Now can you repeat that sequence of movements – forward, back, oh, yes, yes, intriguing; right and left. And now I will just shift one hand to here, so I can sense if there is any pelvic tilt simultaneous with the up and – remarkable, yes, most helpful – and down.

Again?

If you would. It is warm under that sun, isn't it. You have quite a sheen.

My sweat is olive oil.

Now, what if I was to mimic punches being thrown at you? If I stand back here and toss these pebbles at your head, maybe you can show me how you deal with them in a fight? I see. Parrying: arms up, elbows forward, hips ready to rotate. Ducking underneath: arms half up, elbows tucked, jackknifing at the waist. If you could do that motion again, but with my hands on your sacrum? Yes. Yes, I see. Now, this evasion – swaying backwards beyond harm's way. Pubis forward. Very forward. Pelvis tilted far forward to compensate for the backward arch of the upper torso. And that movement again, with my hands now just here and also here? Yes, the controlled compressed power of a great spring, all ready to be uncoiled.

You can feel that?

Yes, I am getting exactly what you are doing. And if I move my hand up here and you do that again? Goodness, that is very much – something.

I do a backflip at the end of each fight.

People must love to see that.

It is a show. Just a brutal variety of show business.

That sun is relentless. I thought perhaps we could cool off in the billabong?

Can you swim in that dress?

Of course not! But as you can see: no one around, and I am no prude.

I'm going to go and find the farmer with the white beard. I am due to fight in Perth soon, and I need bull piss.

We walked all this way – you posed and performed for me – and you want to go and splash about in toilet water instead of having some fun in the billabong with me?

Addio.

37.

So that is what I thought probably happened. You might question how I could be so confident that I could imagine anything from Dora's perspective, but I tell you: no one could have tried harder to see through those eyes of hers. Those mesmerizing eyes. She was a whole different light spectrum. A land all her own.

I asked Grim later for his version of what happened when she went to talk to him.

What are you punching that tree for, she said to me. I said, It helps strengthen my hands. The bones. What has the tree done to you, though, she said. I just looked at her. I think it's not very nice, she said. I've done this to a lot of trees in a lot of different places on two continents and I've never had anyone complain about it, I said.

Where are you from, she said. I told her, and introduced myself, and explained what I do for a living. She said her name was Dora, she was from Albany in the south of the state and now she was a teacher at the local school. She is nineteen and lives at the guest house. I said I could use her local knowledge, and did she know where I could get some fresh bull piss.

Fresh bull piss – what makes you so special, she said. I looked at her again, and she said it was a joke. She said why did I want fresh bull piss. Would salted bull piss do? Was there a particular brand of the canned version I preferred? Or even better, had I ever tried the dehydrated variety? She was a very droll gal. She asked if I needed it for my skin and I asked how she knew and she said her uncle had been a bare knuckle fighter and he swore by ram piss, although he would reuse the one bucket every day for a week or more, he had no qualms about freshness. She said she didn't think there was a bull in town, and when the local cockies wanted to join their heifers they got a stud bull from two towns over. I said, Oh well, I might be able to get some butcher's brine, do they corn the beef locally here or buy it in. She said it was a mutton town, or kangaroo for the poor folks. I don't think the conversation got us anywhere.

I asked if she would take me for a wander around town. We walked past the last house on the last road and out to what she called a billabong. She said she had always been fascinated by fighters and would I teach her some simple moves. I held up my dukes and she put hers up and we play-sparred a little, then I asked her if she knew what a feint was. She said, Is it when you punch to the chin like this, and aimed a straight left at my chin, and as I lifted my hands reflexively, she pulled up short and banged a digging right into my belly. I said, All right, I can't teach you anything. She said she had a lot of boy cousins and she learned to scrap from them.

I suppose I was trying to impress her a little because I told her then my sobriquet, Iron Man, and that I had never been knocked out. She asked to feel my jaw and said, It feels just like a strong fighter's jaw. Why is yours different? I said, I think I am naturally blessed, plus my skull must be thick, plus I have learned to endure and ignore and overcome the pain, plus the training I had head-butting the cathedral door, plus I have some tricks I use. I showed her how I stuck my chin out toward the other fighter, and told her to hit me on the chin, and then when she tried I snapped my head back like a toy on the end of a spring, then I stuck my chin right close to her and stuck my tongue out at her, and she looked cross and tried to swipe my face again, and I pulled my head back, and I said, There, that is one of my tricks. She asked if she could see it again, so I stuck my jaw out inches from her face and wriggled my eyebrows, and she aimed a punch toward me again, but as I pulled back she held that punch short and banged me again into the belly with her other fist. I think you are in the wrong business, I said. [74]

---

74 In *Homo Ludens*, cultural historian Johan Huizinga refers to play as a borderline realm 'between jest and earnest.' Huizinga argued, 'In the

She asked what else I did. I said I tried to control distance, standing just outside the other boxer's reach, or else in so close that their hitting lacked power. Show me, she said. I stepped back, then skipped in close. Of course, you can hug and smother and that can occupy half the time in a fight, I said, perhaps hopefully. No need to show me that one, she said, stepping back. She wanted to know if I had any other tricks. I showed her the big wind-up I gave to my uppercut, telegraphing the punch so much that people always step away, even though the punch rarely lands, just to buy me some time and space. And then I showed her the shimmy I use when I am on the ropes and some monster is whaling on my body, how I pull my arms in tight, elbows tight to my ribs, and I roll my body in a series of crazy-eight shapes, encouraging punches to deflect or slide off me, not providing a square target.

So now I know all your secrets, she grinned. Maybe I'll be the first woman fighter. Oh, I've seen women fight before, I told her. Hideous. Smoke nights, back alley bars, pervert parties. Sometimes in gloves big as pillows so every punch looks ludicrous, fighting in their skimpies or with no tops on at all, and all the men barking. Horrible. Or I've seen coloured women fighting with no gloves, for real, and the dreadful mess they made of lovely faces. Dora just shrugged. And you think it's somehow different for you, she said. Your fight show is okay, but women can't do that. If you have had all those fights and you've never been knocked out, then that means standing up to a preposterous amount of punishment. Maybe I wouldn't want to see you do that. Maybe I'd think it was stupid. Or too horrible.

I am an idiot, I said, I am in the absurdity business, but I am not stupid. I perform a pantomime of pain. I need my audience to

---

form and function of play, itself an independent entity which is senseless and irrational, man's consciousness that he is embedded in a sacred order of things finds its first, highest and holiest expression.'

see how I can suffer, but I don't need to discover that for myself. I know how much punishment my body can withstand: as much as need be. But my audience wants to travel with me on a pain journey, so I give them as much as they need, and for the rest I block blows, I absorb the force of punches through my neck and spine, I stall and distract, I allow myself to be knocked down in order to intensify the spectacle and to wear some extra seconds off the clock. It's a show, and my body is the stage and the instrument, and that is why they pay, and that is how I get to eat well and put money in my name into the bank.

Do you think that is a fair trade-off, though, she said. The gashes? The bruising? The damage those punches might do to your brain? The constant risk of going to work and coming home dead?

I'm pretty okay with it, I said. I think of myself as a travelling artiste. The crowds love me, and then they speak of me once I've gone, and that adds value to my days on the planet, somehow. Now – would you like to have a dip in that billabong? It's a powerfully hot morning.

I don't think so, she said. She said she was not wearing a costume. I tried to charm her. I said where I grew up, no one had a costume. No one had even heard of such a thing. I told her that we could not be seen by prying eyes. I promised not to look, if that would help. I told her that she was very beautiful, which was true, and that I thought she would look even more beautiful paddling in the water, which was also true. I said that I was a gentleman, which was not true.

She asked me if I was married, or if I had a steady girl. My inability to lie tangled me up, as ever. And then she smiled and looked at me with those clever eyes and said, Nice try, though, Joe. She said she would watch me while I swam, but I said I was frightened of snakes, which was true, and we wandered in fair spirits back to town. She said we might be able to borrow horses if I wanted to go on an expedition in search of fresh bull piss, but I admitted I could not ride. She laughed as if I was joking, so I laughed, too. Just as if I was joking. I kept glancing sideways, trying to watch her as she moved inside that thin dress, the uncomplicated, unapologetic way she carried herself, the way each stride landed fractionally further along than anticipated. She noticed me watching her and laughed at me, like I had been caught out, and I was.

38.

As we departed from the guest house and stood at the desk in the wide hallway while the manager strove to total our final amount owing, I saw a beige envelope on the sideboard. It was addressed with a woman's hand to an Albany address, and I grabbed for it as if I was an automaton. Flipped it over. Saw Dora's name on the obverse as sender. I said to the proprietor, I see you have a letter here, I am in fact going very first thing to the box to send mail of my own, would you like me to post this one as well? She seemed to have forgotten how many shillings there are in a pound, was scratching furiously at a selection of numbers, said, Yes, dear that would be most kind, and the envelope was in my pocket.

And, of course, once we had settled up – who will ever know whether we were undercharged, overcharged, we just wanted the ordeal of calcified calculations to end, mouldering there in the front room – and we had made our way to the pickup point for our journey to Perth, without shame and without second thought I slit the envelope with my finger, extracted the floral notepaper, raised it for a moment to my face to smell its perfume, and read the missive that would be kept, deliciously, all for myself for ever.

Dearest darling Esther, my heart,

I miss you so much my sister. Albany is too far, I cannot see your face, and it is altogether thoroughly unfair. Sometimes I am okay and sometimes I miss you so badly it makes my eyes squint.

I know I wrote to you two days ago but I could not wait the full week to tell you about the Most Curious Thing. They say that if you stay in one place for long enough the whole world will eventually come to you, and that is proving true in blessed little Billinup.

This morning I was in my room pondering how best to fill an empty Saturday when my interest was piqued by a repetitive thwacking sound. I went outside and looked in the corner of the yard where the blackbutt stands (do you still have that map I drew you of the guest house layout? The tree is in the back, near the garden shed and the WC) and there was this Most Curious man. He was punching the tree with his bare fists, slowly and methodically, sometimes grunting like an old boar. Then when he tired of that activity he flipped himself upside down, balanced on his head, and rotated his body like some sort of Oriental Acrobat! His head would stay in place but the whole body and limbs would swerve around, he must have the most extraordinary neck muscles!

I sat in the sun and watched him as I finished a letter to Uncle Farquhar. It was then that I noticed we were not alone. There was another man in the yard, and he was watching me the way a black crow looks at a piece of bacon fat. He was not even pretending not to stare, just turned frontally to me and looking in the most blatant and unsettling way. He was an odd man, simultaneously young and old. At one glance he appeared to be about my age, a naive adventurer, and then at the next glance he would be fat with grey hair. I certainly did not request his attention.

Almost to spite this beady fellow I went across to talk to the man exercising beside the blackbutt tree. As I neared him I picked up a most off-putting scent. I think he saw that I recoiled a little, because he said not to mind the smell, he had been soaking in – well, I won't use the words he used, but water made by cattle. For some reason I burst out laughing, and he laughed, too, and the discomfort was averted.

We made our introductions. He is a boxer, born in Italy, domiciled in the United State of America, travelling throughout Australia to compete against our best boys. Can you imagine! He has already fought in Sydney and Melbourne and Zeehan and Ballarat and now he has crossed the entire continent to make a match in Perth! I told him it was an honour for our young state, and he laughed, and I laughed.

Now let me be very specific, dear Esther, this was not a situation of flirting! This was not a man with whom any woman would flirt, let alone your sister! However I liked to talk to him, as it was so exotic to have a prizefighter from America in Billinup – I told him that the only Americans we had ever seen were scruffy miners passing through to the diggings – and I thought I should really put good old W.A. in the best light and try to be hospitable. So I asked if he would like to perambulate around town, and perhaps see the drab billabongs that pass for a Recreational Attraction here! So different to beautiful Albany!

We passed a very pleasant hour. He was polite and told me some blood-curdling yarns about his past fights. He told me the names of the most famous men he has battled, but I did not recognize any of them. He says that he has been in the ring with a Negro who is now World's Champ and he would like to battle him again because that would make an awful lot of money. He has not escaped from his endeavours unscathed. His nose seems almost unmoored from his face, and there are spiderwebs of white scars around his eyes and brow. He said that in some regards he is more akin to a circus performer or a stage actor than a pure sportsman because he uses his body to act a drama for people when he appears.

He asked if I wanted to see how he did what he did. By this time we were at the billabong. I said, 'Yes, by all means, show me your techniques.' He said, 'You will need to see how my body works, it is the only way to pierce the illusion.' I was a little surprised, and then he removed all of his clothing. I was a lot more surprised! I was determined not to betray what I was feeling. I actually felt quite safe at that moment, however thoroughly compromised, but if it was not for the fact that no one ever walks out to the billabongs I would have been blushing even harder than I was.

Remember we used to talk about this at night when we were girls? What it all looks like? Well, I think teachers should be purveyors of knowledge, so I have looked up the relevant pages in the encyclopedia at the Mechanic's Institute Library, I am not embarrassed to say, and I know the rudiments. But I have not been so close to – I will say it – a Member – since swimming with the Wauchope boys when we were tiny. The man – I don't think I have yet given you his name, Mr. Grim – can you imagine that! – said to me, 'Watch my hips as I move.' So, somehow, I couldn't not look! He asked me to toss pebbles at his head and to then watch the way his body moved as he avoided them. He asked me to pretend to punch his head, then he would arc his head backwards into safety like the snap of a whip. He started baiting me, sticking out his tongue to make me want to hit his chin more, so I pretended to aim there and instead socked him in the tummy, it was quite funny, then I thought I had been far too forward.

But he didn't seem to notice – not that, not anything else. He was fully involved with sharing the secrets of his craft. At one point, as I stood at a safe distance, he was expounding on one trick or other that he uses and while he declaimed with right-handed gestures his left hand, can you Believe This, was rotating his Member like a girl twirling a parasol! He did not seem to even notice that he was doing it. I thought perhaps something was going to happen, and I am not completely sure, forgive me, that I would have said no, this being something that has to happen for the first time some time, and perhaps best if I could learn something with a man who is Travelling On. But he didn't ask. He wasn't interested. He seemed fixated only on wanting to talk and communicate his evasions and his endurances.

He asked after a time if the billabong was safe for swimming. I said there were usually snakes around and there was no saying what sort of rubbish had been thrown into that murky water. He asked if I was going to swim. I said I would if he did, and he mused on this, and I mused on what I might do because

I had no costume beneath my dress, but he started speaking again, jabbering really, about the quintessential usefulness of bull water for the skin of his face and hands, and he hauled his garb back on while still jabbering, and we walked back to town, and then he shook my hand vigorously and excused himself as he wanted to go and make enquiries at Methuselah's farm. He was quite the Most unusual man I have ever met! I felt a little dread, returning to the guest house, but Mr. Joe Grim's offsider was nowhere to be seen. I have small doubt that he was spying on me from between some crack in a blind or around an outhouse corner, because that is what men like that do. They are ever so bold within their own minds, then completely cowardly about showing themselves.

No doubt next time I write I will be reduced once again to communicating the vegetable prices at the Billinup Store, reports of which boys have thrown their writing slates out the schoolroom windows, and speculation on the habits clean or otherwise of my landlady, but, dear Esther, This Time there was some real news to savour!

I am, as always, darling girl, your truly loving sister.

Dora

P.S. The beady chap limped past me in the corridor then stopped, introduced himself as if he had not been spying on me all day! I do not trust him a jot.

39.

My uncle, stripes of spilled sherry down his shirt, prowling up and down the word mountain, hurling books full force at my head, spearing paper planes laden with paragraphs at my head, slinging periodicals at my head, stabbing his finger at underlined sentences, shouting his theories and fragments, a slink-hipped tiger of declamatory rage, an ancient creaking man and a wild dog howling.

Look to Terry Eagleton, *The Gatekeeper*: ' … physical pain is a kind of meaninglessness, a brute fact as hard to make anything of as a sneeze. It is just something that happens to you, like belching or falling over your feet; and although there is much to be said about the outworks of it (time off work, hospital visits, saintly or savage nurses), as well as about its causes, location, duration, quality, intensity and potential cure, pain itself is so much the epitome of brute fact that it seems to slip through the nets of language. It is just not part of the order of meaning. It is rather a disruption of meaning, a garbling of sense, a sort of solipsism. It is part of the body's obdurate resistance to intelligibility, its blind, obtuse persistence in its own being. And if pain is meaningless, then so is much of the human history which is saturated by it. In the semiotics of suffering, the abolition of pain is a victory for meaning and a triumph over randomness, even if some postmodern theory sees such randomness, absurdly, as a kind of freedom.'

What is the connection between pain (received) and violence (administered)? Is the latter as utterly pervasive as the former? I am thinking about the most chilling dedication I have ever read, in *Violent Attachments*, the forensic psychiatry handbook written by J. Reid Meloy: 'This book is dedicated to the shadow of violence in our dreams.'

Consider knotty old Nietzsche:[75] 'Thus the Greeks, the most humane people of ancient time, have a trait of cruelty, of tiger-like pleasure in destruction, in them: a trait which is even clearly visible in Alexander the Great, that grotesquely enlarged reflection of the Hellene, and which, in their whole history, and also their mythology, must strike fear into us when we approach them with the emasculated concept of modern humanity. When Alexander has the feet of the brave defender of Gaza, Batis, pierced, and ties his live body to his chariot in order to drag him around to the scorn of his soldiers: this is a nauseating caricature of Achilles, who abused the corpse of Hector at night by similarly dragging it around; but for us, even Achilles' action has something offensive and horrific about it. Here we look into the abysses of hatred.'

Achilles slit Hector's heels and threaded a girdle through the slits, which was then fastened to his chariot. He dragged the body through the Danaan camp, and proceeded to abuse the cadaver for a dozen days. Think of it: a dozen days!

Violence in all of us, violence around all of us. But it is ritualized, fetishized, encapsulated, adumbrated, by the square ring. Thomas Hackett[76] saw it: 'The spectacle of confining two men who had no personal grudge to a small ring and having them beat each other senseless was ... a staged affair – a ritual performance, articulating collective ideals of male will.'

George Bernard Shaw, almost a century earlier: 'Exhibition pugilism is essentially a branch of Art: that is to say, it acts and attracts by propagating feeling. The feeling it propagates is pugnacity. Sense of danger, dread of danger, impulse to batter and destroy what threatens and opposes, triumphant delight in succeeding: this is pugnacity, the great adversary of the social impulse to live

---

75   Homer's Competition

76   *Slaphappy*

and let live; to establish our rights by shouldering our share of the social burden; to face and examine danger instead of striking at it; to understand everything to the point of pardoning (and righting) everything; to conclude an amnesty with Nature wide enough to include even those we know the worst of: namely, ourselves.'[77]

Gerald Early, near the end of the twentieth century, went further: 'The prizefighter enacts a drama of poor taste ... that is in truth nothing more than an expression of resentment or a pantomime of rebellion totally devoid of any political content except ritualized male anger turned into a voyeuristic fetish.'[78]

A fetish with a Janus face, which is pain.

Terry Eagleton described 'that alternative universe which is as close to us as blood and breathing, that inconceivably different place known as agonizing pain into which every moment of our life is potentially a strait gate, and which seems too obscene even for the devil to have created.'[79]

Old-time bareknuckle boxers would be placed on the knees of their seconds between rounds, something almost lovely and unusually intimate, a public expression of male love. It makes me think of the romantic reverberations in the manly swoon of agony, or death. Lay up nearer, brother, nearer for my limbs are growing cold. Kiss me, Hardy.

Toby Miller: 'The sporting body and sex have always been bracketed, by eros, government, or science. In ancient Greece and Rome, the body was the locus for an ethics of self, a combat with pleasure and pain that enabled people to find the truth about themselves and master their drives. Austerity and hedonism could be combined through training. Xenophon, Socrates and Diogenes held that excess

---

77   'Note on Modern Prizefighting'

78   *The Culture of Bruising*

79   *The Gatekeeper*

and decadence came from the equivalent of sporting success. In sex and sports, triumph could lead to failure unless accompanied by regular examination of the conscience and physical training. Carefully modulated desire in both spheres became a sign of fitness to govern others. Aristotle and Plato favoured regular, ongoing flirtations with excess, as tests and as pleasures.' [80]

But sex is not much of interest here. I could pin any sort of sexual fascination on Grim and it would be plausible, or not plausible, and take us no nearer to anything worthwhile. I would rather instead think about Eagleton's thinking, when he adds: 'The form which tries to convert suffering into value is known as tragedy ... For the tragic vision, only by finding our own image in this terrible deformity can we be healed. We must come to pity what we fear, finding in this monstrous travesty of humanity the power to transfigure the human.' [81]

---

80 *Sportsex*

81 *The Gatekeeper*

40.

Coolgardie Miner, 3 July 1909: 'The boxer, Joe Grimm, charged with being of unsound mind, was brought before Mr. Holland, JP, at the Perth Police Court today, and remanded for medical examination. When arrested he struggled so violently that it took the combined efforts of four constables to bring him to the police court buildings.'

Oh no, I said.

Huh? My uncle had moved and was now on top of the eastern bank of books. While dispensing his memories of Dora and Grim in Billinup, he worked with laborious care to build a set of stairs from art texts and hardcover *Wisdens,* then crept to the top of the pile. Pass me up the elixir, he said, and I fetched him what was left of the flagon.

'Unsound mind,' I said.

Oh, that. Tedious. Here, read all about it.

He handed me a photocopy of the single-page entry for Joe Grim in the Claremont Asylum casebook for male patients, Reference: *SROWA consignment 3108 vol 2.*

Joseph Grimm
Date of Admission: 2 July 1909
Age: 27
Religion: RC
Nationality: Italy
M. or S.: Single
Occupation: Pugilist
Friend: [indistinct]
Order by: Aug. S. Roe [Augustus S Roe, Police Magistrate, Perth]
Certified by: Drs Tymms & Deakin
Relatives insane: [blank]

Attack and duration: [blank]
Age on first attack: [blank]
Cause: [blank]
Epileptic: (blank)
Suicidal: [blank]
Height: 5' 8½"
Weight: 12.6
Result: [blank]

Medical certificate
Excitable, restless, noisy & violent, says Police have followed
and poisoned him. Has been dead 4 times. Police are trying to
do away with him. God is talking to him, hears voices under his
pillow, has haematoma auris, very boastful.

Physical condt.
Prominent features many scars on face Degenerate shaped head
high arched palate. Exceptionally well developed Too resistive
for proper medical examination

Mental condt.
When admitted was bound tightly with straps & was very
exhausted & tired. His arms were very swollen & bruised from
where straps had been. He appeared to be frightened & nervous
said that people were trying to poison him & were working
against him. Was very excitable & threatening. Says he is God
etc & is exalted [this word possibly incorrect]

July 3rd
Given a bed in single room, was very violent & resistive &
homicidal

July 4th
Patient required six attendants to put him in single room. He
[word looks like 'seemed' but could be 'seized'] nozzle of fire

hose & threatened to kill attendants. In the struggle his leg was badly bruised. Placed for 10 [appears to have '11' written over the top] hours in straightjacket.

July 6th
Very cunning & plausible. When resistive he kicks & bites & has destroyed the clothes of several of the attendants

July 10th
Still very uncertain. Now sleeping in the ward

July 17th
Improving. Does not express delusions now.

July 25th
Not so well for past few days. Delusions returned

Aug 1st
Improving again.

Aug 20th
Very much better

Aug 26th 1909
Discharged Recovered

41.

Claremont Asylum was a brooding presence in a suburb of Perth, managed by the Lunacy Department under the stewardship of the Inspector General of the Insane, administering the Lunacy Act of 1903. It was a new facility, with a farm, an orchard, and pleasant grounds, but the two-storey building, constructed of red brick and Donnybrook stone, was secure as any jail.

What did I do for the forty-five days Grim was confined there? I wafted in and out of the picture. I mooned over my carefully constructed vision of the disappeared Dora. I read, and every new thing I read seemed more pertinent than the last, and I wondered if I would ever develop a thought of my own.

I thought of R. D. Laing's description of the skull as the Golgotha of the spirit,[82] and all the endless unwinnable battles that are waged inside that treacherous garden. I thought of the Spartans whose society functioned with bristling brilliance while at war, but dissolved into mess when peace arrived because they had no capacity to deal with ease and leisure, and I wondered how this might apply to other warriors, such as boxers, such as Joe Grim.

I thought of pain, a lot. I thought of C. S. Lewis calling pain 'God's chisel.'[83] I thought of notes my uncle must once have made about Buddhism that suggest that pain is part of life's curriculum, and that we suffer pain because that is what happens to human bodies in this world. I thought of another note about Hindu sage Ramana Maharshi's prolonged time with terminal cancer; at night he would scream in agony and say, 'There is pain, but there is no

82   *Wisdom, Madness and Folly*

83   *The Problem of Pain*

suffering.'[84] I think of my own fear of pain, which is in truth a fear of not being able to endure.

I thought of incarceration, in whatever brand of institution, and Sade biographer Maurice Lever's insight: 'Inside the prison walls history comes to a halt; time's mechanism goes awry. The prisoner is suddenly plunged into "uchronia," into a world where time does not exist.'[85] I think of my own fear of imprisonment in jail or asylum; again, it is primarily a fear of not being able to endure pain without limit.

But otherwise I just lingered outside the asylum walls, soaking up the winter sun and letting the westerlies blow me this way and that, and waiting to be invited in to speak with Grim. I was only permitted access when he was in phases of lucidity. Some of the warders muttered darkly about his behaviour when he was less than tractable, less than pleasant, but what were they going to do – hit him?

84   B. V. Narashima Swami, *Self Realization: Life & Teachings of Sri Ramana Maharshi*

85   *Sade: A Biography*

42.

Evening News, Sydney, 27 August 1909
Joe Grimm, the boxer, who was recently remanded for medical examination, has been removed to the Claremont Lunatic Asylum. He struggled desperately this morning when requested to enter the vehicle to take him to Claremont, and shrieked at the top of his voice that the police were trying to murder him. It was necessary to strap his arms and legs.

I[86] am Joe Grim and I fear no man.

I am Joe Grim and I fear no man.

I am Joe Grim, I am Joe Grim and I fear no man.

I am Joe Grim, I am Joe, Grim, and I fear no man.

I am Joe Grim, I am, Joe, Grim, and I fear no man.

I am Joe I am Joe Grim. I am Joe Grim and I fear no fear no man.

I am Joe. I am Joe Grim. I fear no Joe Grim. I fear. No.

I fear no. I fear. I Joe Grim. I am. I fear.

I am Joe Grim. I am Joe Grim. I am Joe Grim.

I fear no fear Joe fear no man Joe Grim. I am no fear.

I am no fear. I no Joe Grim. I fear no am. I am Joe Grim.

I Grim. I fear. I am. I Grim. I fear. I am. I Grim.

I am Joe Grim I fear no fear.

I am.

---

86 There is a sound poem by the great Jas H. Duke, easy to find online, called 'No, No You Can't Do That.' While I wrote this I played it on a loop for hours: 'No, no you can't do that. Nonoyoucan'tdothat. No, no, no, no,   . you can't do that. NO, NO, you can't do that. NO-NO-YOU-CAN'T-DO-THAT. No, no, no, no, no, no, NO you can't do that. No, no you can't do that. No, no you can't do THAT. No, no … ' and et cetera.

I man. I Grim Joe fear. I am no and.

Joe Grim. Joe fear. No Grim. No Grim.

A bell is struck, somewhere.

What does the word *Eucharist* mean?

I am unsure.

I fear I am my own Eucharist.

Is that all you fear?

All I said was I fear no man.

That leaves plenty of scope, yeah.

They bound me in calico. Leather straps. Metal buckles. White rope. It was the worst experience of my life.

They said they had to. They said you were a danger to staff and a danger to yourself.

That is what they say.

But you're unshackled now. The attendant told me you're free to walk in the garden with supervision.

What use is a garden for me? I do not make things grow. Things blossom, things bloom, things fruit or branch or ripen in a garden, but I am only of value for the world of destruction. We take the most beautiful thing, and we destroy it, and we do it for show, and we do it for money. I can't belong in a garden.

Perhaps this career is coming to an end. [87] There must be more

---

87   "'I always wanted you to admire my fasting," said the hunger artist.
"But we do admire it," said the supervisor obligingly. "But you shouldn't admire it," said the hunger artist. "Well then, we don't admire it," said the supervisor, "but why shouldn't we admire it?" "Because I had to fast. I can't do anything else," said the hunger artist. "Just look at you," said the supervisor, "why can't you do anything else?" "Because," said the hunger artist, lifting his head a little and, with his lips pursed as if for a kiss, speaking right into the supervisor's ear so that he wouldn't miss anything, "because I couldn't find a food which I enjoyed. If had found that, believe me, I would not have made a spectacle of myself and would

to you than simply an iron chin.

Of course there is. There is the dancing dago, the loco eyetie, the barking tumbling southern European circus dog who makes cruel men laugh. I am a pantomime dame in eight-ounce leather gloves. I do these things, and then I stand in front of the hardest hitting men on the planet, and then the promoter still tries to – do you know this Australianism? – fuck me sideways on fight payments as I make my way home. It is a pitiful racket and I have been in it too long, and I have no other path ahead, and that is that is that.

A bell is struck, somewhere.

I have worries. Can I tell you that I have worries? So many worries. They – in fact everything – slip through my brain like minnows flitting through shark nets. Do you know the oh-no sensation of something slipping your mind that you were about to say; well, I have that sensation seventy times a minute; each thought enters my brain and is shunted out before I can think it, left here only watching the departing procession of thoughts that remain unrecognized, and then another one, and then another one, and then another one. It is very subtle and very real torture. But some of the worries linger, imposed over the top of the fleeing floating phantasms. I worry that I am outside the scope of nature. I am not just at the edge of my species, but over the margin. I do not belong. I worry that one day my fighting might end, and that without the pain I will have no map to find myself. I worry that men laugh when I am performing a tragedy. I worry sometimes that I am actually Christ.

A bell is struck, somewhere.

I'm glad you said you would sit with me in the garden.

---

have eaten to my heart's content, like you and everyone else.'" Franz Kafka, 'The Hunger Artist'

I have told you: I have no use for gardens, nor them me. I told you that, and again you did not want to hear. I lose power in nature! Too much open air drains my power and I am then like any other man. When I am not any other man! I am Joe Grim. I exist beyond the realm of the human possible. I need to be inside! Suck my vitality from where there is no air, no light. Build my majesty. Indomitable creature of wall and hearth. I am Joe Grim, the mighty, and I alone fear no depth of darkness.

A bell is struck, somewhere.

One reason they chose this site for the asylum, apparently, is the artesian water supply, I said, which handily reminds me of a joke. There is a bloke who is way out in the sticks, travelling around, and he stops one day at a pig farm. The farmer says, Come on in and have a feed, cobber. We don't get many visitors out this way. The bloke says, No worries, thank you kindly. They sit down and the farmer says, We've got plenty to eat. I can offer you ham, bacon, pork, or trotters. What takes ya fancy? The bloke says, It all sounds fine, you beauty, and I wouldn't mind something to drink. The farmer apologizes and says, All we've got to drink out here, mate, is bore water. And the bloke – you'll like this – the bloke replies, Geez, you fellas don't waste any bit of the pig, do ya.

I understand. The humour hinges on the confusion of bore and boar. Of course, it would not work quite so effectively in Italian. Alesaggio acqua does not correspond well to cinghiale acqua. Although possibly that would make the joke funnier.

A bell is struck, somewhere.

What when I can't box no more? What when in that then? In that boxing time, I am outside of time. Six rounds, three minutes each, and in that span I belong to that span only. There is no connection to clock time, to earth time. And that is how I live, with and for those ripped-out portions where time has no dominion. Six three-minute rounds, five one-minute breaks, twenty-three minutes that are as long as you need them to be, or they can be devoid of time altogether, black holes in a lifetime that expand and contract as needed, both being and nothingness.

I pledged my self to this life of three minutes and one minute and three minutes, always time defined, and if I survive through the six rounds and I always do, the reward is monetary and the reward is also another parcel of time-that-is-not-time, a neat portion of chronological space in which I do not have to submit to the ticking and the tocking. Same for twelve rounds, same for twenty. Same, only longer. I know this has wrought damage, I know I am not as I should could be, but I signed up to this a long time ago and the damage if not its own reward is not the damnation some might think.

Some might think, some might think. I had some, a person or persons or perhaps it was just me, trying to say that the glory of pain is that it teaches you things. And I say as one who might know, if there is enough of it then pain is just pain. Yes it abstracts and swirls into shapes, oil on water, but a lot of pain is a lot of pain and it is not a friend and not a teacher and not a guide and not a redemption. It is just pain. Six rounds, twelve rounds, twenty rounds: three minutes each, pain, eye-blinding pain, outside of time, a parcel a portion a package of non-ness of not-ness, liberation through negation, six times three plus five times one, or twelve times three plus eleven times one, or twenty times three and nineteen times one, and Grim still standing declared the winner of his own uniquely defined contest, pay up now please as I hurtle back into the time-world.

A bell is struck, somewhere.

Do you know depression, I said. The main characteristic of depression is that you are stuck. You are without agency, without motive force, you cannot move to a state of optimism or rouse to take any action – no matter how trivial – that may improve your lot because depression is a mire and you are stuck neck deep. But madness is madness. It is a train leaving the rails far behind and plowing through wheatfields through harbourfront houses through birthday parties through religious ceremonies through swimming pools through lovers through fathers through any sense of sense through last shreds of rationality through good decisions through bad decisions through any decisions through the colour blue and the colour red, through symphonies and through snarls and through all the bends that can be found in light that are invisible to any other eye. Madness is just madness and should make no greater claim. [88] But the opposite of madness is not what you think, not sanity; the opposite of madness is responsibility, and madness is a respite from that fierce overlord. You need to be brave and come back to the world.

I am thinking of a chunk of bread, and poor-grade boot leather, said Grim. A chunk of bread, poor-grade boot leather. That is what I thinking. I thinking bread, a chunk, and boot leather: poor-grade. Poor-grade boot leather and a chunk of bread. That is what I thinking, now.

A bell is struck, somewhere.

I am Joe Grim and I fear no man.
I fear no man I am Joe Grim
I am Joe Grim, and I fear no man. I am Joe Grim.
I am Joe Grim, I am Joe, Grim, and I fear no man.
I am Joe Grim, I no fear, I Joe Grim, I am and I am.
I am Joe I am Joe Grim. I am Joe Grim and I fear no fear no man.
I am Joe. I am Joe Grim. I fear no Joe Grim. I fear. No.

---

88 'I could have been mad of course, but there's no point in explaining madness.' Brian Castro, *The Bath Fugues*

I fear no. I fear. I Joe Grim. I fear, I Grim.

I fear no fear Joe fear no man. Joe Grim, I am no fear.

I am no fear. I no Joe Grim. I fear no am. I am Joe Grim.

I Grim. I fear. I am. I Grim. I fear. I am. I Grim.

I am Joe Grim! I fear no fear!

I am.

A chunk of bread, and poor-grade boot leather.

No, no you can't do that.

Chunk bread. Poor-grade boot. Leather.

Joe Grim. Joe fear. No Grim. No Joe. No fear no Joe no Grim.

43.

Vancouver Daily World, 27 August 1909
Recent advices from Australia state that Grim, who has been considered mentally unbalanced for some time, recently became a howling maniac and had to be placed in a lunatic asylum in Perth, West Australia.

Last fall Grim worked his way to Australia, and after his arrival there was considered the ripest kind of a lemon in the Antipodean pugilistic world.

For a time, prior to the historic Burns-Johnson fight, Joe Grim was in Tommy Burns' training quarters, acting as a sort of human punching bag for the Canadian champion. It is said on one occasion that Burns knocked Grim down nineteen times in three rounds and then owned up to a helpless feeling when Grim came up laughing, and poked his chin at him.

'Hanged if I knew what to do with him,' Tommy is reported to have said. 'He was the easiest mark in the world to hit, as he had absolutely no defence, but he certainly could take punishment that would put out any ordinary good heavyweight, and come back smiling for more.'

Vancouver Daily World, 11 September 1909
Ten thousand miles from home and friends, Joe Grim, the veritable punching bag, now weak and destitute, is languishing under constant guard, an inmate of the Claremont lunatic asylum, at Perth, Australia. Time, which plays no favourites, has finally succeeded where all the ring champions of the world have tried and failed.

Grim, the iron-jawed marvel of the age, and the despair of the scientists, who have frequently examined him in a vain effort to fathom the secret of his phenomenal strength, has given way beneath the strain of several years, consistent punishment and is now declared hopelessly insane.

There is sufficient substantiation to the stories to warrant the belief that Joe Grim's fighting days are forever over, and if he is eventually able to secure his release from the Australian asylum, he will be a pathetic contrast to his former massive self.

For the past few weeks he has demonstrated signs of failing mentality. Because of his unsettled condition the promoters were unwilling to provide him with matches. He had been acting queerly and the authorities made several examinations before they finally decided to place him in the asylum for the insane.

It is the opinion of the Australian specialists who have examined him that the terrific lacings to which he has been subjected in recent years have finally told on him. His frequent contact with the fists of his slugging opponents has confused the grey matter, and it is a safe conclusion that he will never regain his former strength.

Sydney Sportsman, 15 September 1909
Our Fremantle correspondent telegraphs that Joe Grim, well-known pugilist, who for some weeks past has been an inmate of the hospital, has now recovered. He is returning to Sydney, and left by the R.M.S. *Orient* on Thursday.

HE
What pain?
SHE
The pain of being present.
– Philip Roth, *Exit Ghost*

44.

My uncle had paused frequently in the telling, distracted by the work of scooping a ditch in the top of the east bank of words on paper. He was breathing hard. He used the displaced items to build a low wall around his ditch, then used ancient atlases and other large volumes to build a partial roof. Satisfied with his construction, he eased himself inside the shallow shelter and grinned with eerie contentment. He lapped at the sherry flagon. Closed his eyes.

I should leave you, I said.

Why?

You've told me plenty. That is an end to the story, such as it is. And it's time for you to rest.

Stories don't end. You know that. They don't arc. They don't do anything, except meander and continue and spin and wait to be rediscovered.

Okay. But I don't need any more.

There is only a little. Grim kept his date with Bob Fraser in Perth and the fight was judged a draw. Then the R.M.S. *Orient* back to the eastern states. Lobbying for fights in Melbourne. Sparring exhibitions for cash with Jack Williams at the Gaiety Athletic Club in Sydney. Calling out Mike Williams for a rematch, a provocation to which Williams did not respond. He saw more of the continent than most natives. Fought in every state except South Australia. When he left New South Wales for the last time, bound for a final fight in Charters Towers, a Mr. Unholz took up a collection from Sydney boxers to tide him over. A generous gesture, far kinder than the *Kalgoorlie Sun* one week earlier, which gabbled: 'The *Referee*'s boxing scribe says he doesn't believe that Grimm was ever mad whilst he was in this State! The writer should have heard

Joe when he was being taken from the Roe-street lock-up to the Claremont Asylum!'[89]

Yeah. That is no easy stain to escape. Leastwise from yourself.

When he left Australia there were still a few adventures ahead. He got himself to Paris, where he had one fight, and then back to the U.S.A. for twenty more fights, according to the official record. He was KO'd in a couple of them, mainly against ham-and-eggers but including one bout against a genuine top-runger, the handsome Battling Levinsky at the old Broadway Athletic Club in Philly. And then, in his third-last bout, against a debutant called Kid Ramsey, Grim upset all applecarts by winning the fight on points. Kid Ramsey never fought again. Grim retired in 1913 and was shut up in an asylum for three years. He was released in 1916, worked on the docks in New York, then was locked away again in the Philadelphia State Hospital for Mental Diseases and did not die until 1939. There is a photo[90] of him, with two years left to live, dressed in a preposterous bib shirt and bow tie at a dinner for the Veteran Boxers Association. You notice two things. Firstly, that his one visible eye stares far off and might as well be made of glass. Secondly, that the angle of the hand holding the spoon that is in his mouth suggests it is not his own hand. Grim, aged fifty-five, is almost certainly being fed like an infant. Did the hand belong to his wife, Carrie? A carer, from the State Hospital for Mental Diseases? Or another old boxer who understood?

That's a long twilight.

Maybe his twilight started earlier. It is hard for me to know. I was a young man when I was with him. I did not know what I know now: all those things that you can only know with years.

And so the story ends.

---

89   Quoted in *Sydney Sportsman*, 6 October 1909

90   Accompanying his obituary, *Philadelphia Inquirer*, 19 August 1939

Have you been listening? Stories don't end. I stopped thinking so much about Grim, and boxing, and that particular variety of pain, when he departed our shores. I had other hares to chase. But the story didn't disappear just because I stopped paying attention. The solitary Paris fight – a loss, of course – was with the magnificent Sam McVea [91] who, despite his brilliance, could not stop Grim over twenty stanzas. What else happened in France for Grim, though? Did he promenade and drink coffee and carouse in nightclubs and visit Gertrude and Leo? Did he make a side trip to Italy and meet forgotten relatives? Was he well? Was he locked up again? How did he make money? Do you care?

---

91 McVea followed the Grim encounter with a healthy string of wins in France, Geneva, and the United Kingdom before crossing to the opposite face of the globe and arriving in Sydney. He had four fights in his first four months in Australia and won them all, including a KO demolition of Bill Lang. Then there was an astounding chain of fights against Sam Langford, the Boston Tar Baby, perhaps one of the best ten fighters to ever lace a glove. Two black men duking it out in Sydney (four times), Perth, and then Brisbane for the Australian Heavyweight Title as well as the World Colored Heavyweight Championship – because, bitter irony of ironies, Jack Johnson maintained the 'colour bar' and did not fight a black opponent for the first five years of his world heavyweight title reign. Langford and McVea travelled together around Australia. What sort of reception did they receive? What did they do apart from fighting? We know that Langford made paid appearances narrating film of one of his victories. But what else? McVea went to the Rink Hall in Lismore in November 1913 and fought an 'all in' bout against local ju-jitsu exponent Professor P. W. Stevenson. The Prof locked in painful submission holds to win each of the first four rounds, but in the fifth McVea dropped him three times, then finished him on the ground with (legal) blows to the back of the neck. Within a year some of the young Lismore men watching this strange event would be wearing khaki and preparing to sail overseas to their death. Did they practise Professor Stevenson's arm bars and chokeholds on each other while roughhousing on deck during the long journey to Europe? Did they tell tales of the magnificent African-American McVea and liken his lethal finishing punches to what they planned to unleash on the Turks? Perhaps. Or not.

Well, a little, I said. But I can only hear so much. Is that our conclusion? Is there anything more about Joe Grim in Australia? You know I'm most grateful.

Here are your four tenets to take out into the darkness, and damn the gratefulness bullshit, my uncle said. He handed me a yellowed scrap of loose-leaf on which was inscribed – perhaps with a quill? – the following:

That which opposes fits.
    – Heraclitus

Strife is the source and the master of all things.
    – Heraclitus

Art is a wound turned into light.
    – George Braque

Death is the fighter's only exit.
    – Seneca

Okay, I said.

Okay, he said, gargling sherry and then spitting it back into the bottle. You can't go until you've heard about Charters Towers. Just let me get comfortable here and sort out how it all transpired. Okay, he said. Okay:

45.

The banks of the Burdekin. Grim, as always, did not want to get to town too far ahead of time. We numbered four. Grim and me, plus the goat and the gold standard of manliness, old Saitchell. The goat was waiting for us when we docked at Townsville and grumbled every step of the way as we struck inland toward Charters Towers. Leave me alone out there! Middle of the fucken desert! Every man for his fucken self and fuck the goat to hell why don't ya! The goat said it had been hard trying to keep track of Joe through the wire services. He walked all the way to Kalgoorlie only to get word that Grim had re-emerged in Sydney. Very fucken inconvenient, he said. We were possibly glad to see the goat again but chose not to make this known.

Saitchell didn't say where he was going to or coming from. He stopped at our camp, such as it was, and asked if an old timber cutter could avail himself of a little company for an evening, and we said yes, and then he didn't leave and we didn't suggest it. Apart from anything else he was clever at catching eel-tailed catfish and scooping up mud crabs, a drastic improvement on the dirt-water damper that had been our staple. The goat thought we made too much noise about Saitchell's food provision. It's a very big fucken river and I think you will find there are black catfish, eastern rainbowfish, empire fucken gudgeon, mangrove jack, Agazziz's glassfish, tilapia, yellowbelly, freshwater longtom, and even fucken barramundi, said the goat, fuck me backwards, the Burdekin is roiling with banded grunter if you must know, but all hail the ancient bushwhacker who can snaffle a few bottom-dwellers and crabs that move slower than Grim's footwork. We ignored the goat and picked our teeth each lazy night with sweet white catfish bones.

Saitchell, who had travelled, was familiar with Grim's work. He had been in Philadelphia in 1903 doing some stevedoring when Grim constructed his Peerless Tetralogy over a span of three months and four days. That was when Grim fought Peter Maher (a former heavyweight champion of the world; when he met Grim, the great Maher boasted a record of 128 wins, 15 losses, and 5 draws), Joe Walcott (welterweight champion of the world, then 80–11–15), Bob Fitzsimmons (heavyweight champion of the world, 63–9–13), and Joe Gans (lightweight champion of the world, 131–7–16). No man ever tackled world champions across three weight divisions in four straight fights, and no one will again.

Add it up, Saitchell said, those bastards had more than four hundred wins between them and not one of the bludgers could finish you off. Who was the best?

All of them. Gans was good. Johnson was good. But none good enough.

The black fighters were better then.

Don't care if they're black, don't care if they're white. Big punchers mean big crowds mean more moolah.

What I wanted Grim to say instead was: I crave interesting challenges, from opponents black, green, or brindle. I have no time for racism and abhor those who promulgate it. Take Tommy Burns, for example, who was both excoriated and praised for breaking the 'colour bar' when he fought Johnson. Well, Burns showed his true colours when Joe Gans fought George Memsic. Burns crouched in Memsic's corner and howled abuse all night.[92] You wouldn't know that Burns knew Gans had a name; he was the coon, the dinge, the smoke, boogie. Gans won on points, effortlessly, and I thought every jab he twisted into poor Memsic's face was a retort to Burns in the opposing corner. Myself, I want my opponent to be greater, not

---

92   William Gildea, *The Longest Fight: In the Ring with Joe Gans, Boxing's First African American Champion*

diminished, because that makes me greater. That was the speech I wished I could hear from Grim, but it was my speech and never his.

I thought after the asylum your insights might extend a bit deeper, I said.

Grim turned to me, eyes grey in a face that had tanned to the colour of a drover's boot heel. I know why I'm here. What about you? Still running away?

It'll be a woman he's running from, said the goat. Or more fucken likely a man.

Saitchell said nothing, just raised one eyebrow a sixteenth of an inch.

It's modern fucken times, said the goat. Chase all the blokes you want, fucken good onya.

It's not a bloke, I said. And not a woman, either. I know I can't use another human to solve my problems.

Fucken knew it, said the goat. You're after some goat action. Well, get to the back of the fucken queue.

I'll cook some more of those eel-tailed catfish for everyone, said Saitchell, and the goat rolled his eyes and muttered something unpleasant.

You want a flag you can march behind, said Grim. You could do worse than attach yourself to Saitchell.

Well, I never wanted to be Ned Kelly, I said. I wanted to be Joe Byrne.

Most men want to be spear carriers, said Grim. Harder to be the one out front on your own.

There's a trick to life, I reckon, said Saitchell, positioning the twitching fish over the fire. I think you'll find it, even if you have to wait until you're very old. Just keep looking. You'll probably get there in the end.

46.

It is not so hard to sleep when your bed is the lap of night blanketed by the ancient muttering of water moving ineluctably from land to ocean. Is this the oldest sound of all? Slow, solemn, the steady decline into somnolence. And so we slept. There were night birds, and the wriggle of reptiles in sand and riverbank bush, and human snoring, and sometimes the conversation of distant livestock, but it was all swathed in river sigh, and the mosquitoes and heat prickle did not stop us drifting, and our sleep was like the river as well: that shut-eye state where all the dread heart stones carried through wake time are without weight or consequence.

We slept. Men on a riverbank. All over the world men were sleeping on riverbanks, all part of a single endless river, one vast family drifting through sleep to the susurration of one river, all doing our best to get through days, all seeking respite at night from fears and terrors smothered and smoothed by sleep, sleep induced by the sound of solemn water moving from land to sea, from land to sea, the endless ancient movement a loop without start or end. Men asleep, their troubles neatly folded and placed beneath their heads, placated by river whisper murmur rush or rumble. We slept.

And then we didn't. A stockwhip crack, loud as the world splitting apart. I struggle-swum from dream's depths toward consciousness, lost in the deep blue, and panicked suddenly, stupidly groping for surface lost and maybe too distant, just for that piece of then, and then breaking the meniscus into wake reality, hitting like a blare of trumpet. Awake then, knowing there had just been a stentorian sound, guessing initially it was a widow-maker branch splitting from a gum tree.[93] I looked at Grim, and the goat, and Saitchell,

93 Beloved Judy in *Seven Little Australians* always dying again in memory.

and saw that they were not pinned to the riverbank beneath a lethal section of eucalypt. It was not a tree branch. The crack that zagged us from deep sleep to consciousness was followed by a bellowed *Ha!* and another crack, and then horse snort, foaming muzzle, too-loud toccata of hooves, familiar sounds far too close. It was pre-dawn but summer had started and night at that time is never completely night, and the others were woken and upright, and so we had a fair view of what was coming, rendered in deep blues and blacks, and the snarling savage soundtrack that temporarily obliterated all river sounds.

Ha! shouted Pig Thug, a blubbery naked grotesque on a high-step-ping Arabian horse. *Ha!* Flourishing a stockwhip that looked longer than the Burdekin. *Ha! Crack. Ha!* In front of his swingeing whip and his roiling head-tossing Arabian and his quivering alabaster jelly carcass was a swarm of feral pigs. Boars and sows, the stink carrying in front of them like a bow wave, rotted meat and diseased fangs, death, and you could see tusks on the males, red eyes like paired simulacra of the planet Mars in the night sky, rampaging toward our camp.

A wasp-angry coven of feral pigs being driven through our campsite by a naked grotesque on a hoof-flinging horse. The corpse stink of feral pig breath, sweat with stench of poison secreted through every needle-bristle pore, the death-stink washing across us, a shroud that might never be shrugged off, *Ha!* from Pig Thug and he wheeled the vile beasts and then drove them back hard through the centre of our campsite, hooves and stink, devastating our makeshift beds and provisions, one disease-dripping razorback stomping straight though the middle of our campfire, the clatterclang of our billy kicked away and trampled, a fine white cloud of ash thrown up and dusting the scene like northern Christmas snow. Pig Thug jammed his curled toenails – sharp as spurs, hardened over candles, useful for plucking out eyes – into the flanks of his steed and rocketed forward, careening high up the riverbank and downriver until he headed the surging pig stampede, and then the savage smack of his serpentine stockwhip, and he wheeled them again, a perfect volte-face, and *Ha!* and they lurched like grapeshot hitting a wall and rampaged back through our camp, stinking feral hooves tangled in bag straps and spare garments and flour bags and boxes of tea and tobacco and notebooks and pens and photos of loved ones and amulets and every meagre possession of travelling men of limited means, the razorback plowing back through the fire again, smart nimbus of red embers fanned out through blue-black pre-dawn, the gut-choking stink of those monsters, and then the worst stinking monster of all, Pig Thug, reaching one naked sweat-drenched arm toward me from high on his noble Arabian and grabbing me around the throat and lifting me and hissing, snake voice and snake breath, the stink of blighted eternity, hissing: 'You will never be free of this, you will never not be that frightened little boy, never not be that useless unwanted outsider, no, not ever,' and then flexing his corpulent arm and flicking me backwards and laughing as I fell agonizingly into splayed ashes, busted valuables, feral pig shit. He whirled the whip above me and cracked it so hard that I could not hear the sound, could only feel the air as it was abused by the cruel snarling greenhide, and he raked the steed's midriff with his sabre toenails and trotted off.

I gestured helplessly to my comrades. The fuck was all that, said the goat. I thought Saitchell would have been stomped by the feral swarm, but he was untouched, just limped off and found the billy and used his fist to hammer it back into shape, scooped it full of Burdekin water and started reconstructing the fire.

There was no sign of Grim.

I could not properly feel my legs, did not know for sure where my feet were in relation to the ground. My mouth and my throat tasted of smoke and fear and the stench of malevolent pig. I sat dumb in the heaved-up sand beside the dismembered fire and watched Saitchell and his patience and tried to think about breathing in and out.

Nice fucken friends you've got, said the goat.

No friend of mine, I said, and realized that was redundant.

Then we spotted Grim, upside down with his torso twisting and legs swinging, going through his calisthenic routine beside the broad brown Burdekin. After a time he brushed himself down and rejoined the camp. Nice friends you've got, he said to me.

Not actually a friend of mine, not sure why I have to keep saying this, I said. I notice you didn't stay around to help me out.

Not about me, said Grim. You keep saying my story is about the idea of suffering, the long and pointless parabola of a career fighting for money, exchanging pain for a living wage, meditations on masculinity, the acceptance of slings and arrows, my lonely brutal samadhi, et cetera. The other stuff about irrelevant childhood bullies and unexceptional brain terrors that recur at an unseemly late age, that's not me. You haven't thought to just move on? Lock those people somewhere in the past? You really see value in dragging them around the world wherever you go?

I'll think about it, I said.

No time like the fucken present, said the goat.

Give the kid a chance, said Saitchell. A man does what he does. And no life is easier to lead than the other person's. It's getting your own life straight that is hell difficult.

Some of us do it, said Grim, and I disliked him right then. I didn't mention Claremont.

I think I am getting close to something, I said. I am just having trouble making out what it is.

The end, Saitchell said. You're getting closer to the end. He threw a handful of tea leaves into the billy, stirred it briefly with a eucalyptus leaf, and went to wash feral pig flop off the enamel pannikins. The sun crept higher, the goat stretched and yawned and shut its eyes for a while, then Grim and I accepted the mugs of bush tea and we let the day emerge.

You know, I said, if it wasn't for all the honour, glamour, and riches it's brought me, I would prefer to have missed out on mental illness. In my next life, when you have to choose your afflictions, I will tick Anything Else.

Fabulous that you're no longer prone to self fucken pity, said the goat. Your attitude stinks like those feral boars. You could learn plenty about attitude from me. I know for a fact it will be eel-tailed catfish for the next ten meals, but I still choose to think a banded grunter might leap out of the shallows and land neatly in the ashes of our fire. And it will carry several slices of lemon in its back. But fuck me, what would I fucken know. I'm just the fucken goat.

Which actually made me laugh. I sucked at my strong tea and thought about mental illness and self-delusion and Grim and how it all might slot together. Every fighter lies to himself. Slipping through the ring ropes, holding up your fists for money, convincing yourself that the animal in the other corner cannot or at least will not kill you, ignoring lopsided measurements in height or reach or age or experience, pretending that a show of heart or some rare good luck will erase the disparity in talent: these self-delusions are as integral to a fighter's kit as gloves and a groin protector. The fighter does not need to be insane, but in the absence of useful insanity there must be a furious willingness to fool oneself. Otherwise the potential repercussions of letting another man try to hit your head as often as they can with as much force as they can would compel a rational being to rather juggle knives or kiss taipans.

The sport has always been abysmally violent. No use pretending. After Jem Burn's thrashing by Ned 'White-Headed Bob' Baldwin in 1826 it was reported that 'every feature was literally knocked out of him.'[94] Lest it be thought that only modern boxers struggle with life outside the ring, the same book records that when the boxer Bendigo was drunk he was easily angered. 'I have heard of his stripping a butcher's shop on one such occasion, and flinging the joints one after another at the crowd who were jeering at him.' Grim was not an originator, but an apotheosis: this infernal man who couldn't win but wouldn't be beaten, at least in terms of the contest as he constructed it.

Or so I understood it all, as the sun flared higher and Saitchell doused the outer edges of the firepit, looking to maintain a few embers for boiling water but no longer wanting to add to the ambient heat. I picked at my teeth with a catfish bone and stared at the sky and thought a long time about writing, and the lies all writers tell themselves, and that one thing makes as little sense as another, really.

---

94   Thormanby (pen name of W. Willmott Dixon), *Boxers and Their Battles: Anecdotal Sketches and Personal Recollections*

47.

'(Modern writing) consists in gumming together long strips of words which have already been set in order by someone else, and making the results presentable by sheer humbug.'
George Orwell, 'Politics and the English Language'

The Northern Miner, Charters Towers, 7 December 1909
CORRESPONDENCE
Dear Sir, – I feel that I cannot rest without taking this, my first opportunity of expressing myself and showing the people of Charters Towers that as well as being a pugilist, I am a gentleman, and an honest one. I was fully prepared to go on with the fight, although the house was so meagre, but my manager and the opposing parties would not hear of me stripping. All I wanted to do is, what is honest and straightforward. As you know yourself, I have fought all over the world and have borne and still bear a good reputation. I will fight Regan on Thursday, and all who come to see me fight can rest assured that I will fight till the death and give of my very best. The sportsmen of Charters Towers will understand how I have myself been greatly inconvenienced inasmuch as I had every hope of fighting the winner of the Bill Turner–Pat O'Keefe fight in Sydney, and the delay may make a great difference to my future prospects. I will call on you and explain matters fully and show the people of this city that I will do the right thing by them. I will conclude by saying that in this, as in every other large mining centre, one meets the best sports and wants to treat them properly. Thanking you for your past favours – Yours very sincerely, Joe Grimm.[95]

---

95   Grimm, rather than Grim – the same error as when his name was recorded in the Claremont Asylum record book. Did he perhaps dictate

his letter to a baffled journo at the *Northern Miner*, and they made this small mistake with his name at the writing or the typographical stage? Or was he perhaps identifying differently by this point, Grimm a subtly different person to Grim? Still Grimmish, though, old Saverio.

48.

Charters Towers was Queensland's second largest city, bustling and confident. In the afternoon I followed Grim into Lissner Park where he was hardening his knuckles against an African mahogany. This tree, like others around it, was choked with bats caterwauling, flinching their wings, climbing over each other, the sound and smell insistent and maddening, like rotten fruit come alive. Hot stink of bat: fox pelt and dog piss and red peppercorns. Damn fruit bats are killing all the trees, said the slow-talking park dweller in bowyangs and cabbage tree hat. You know the only thing that works: you have to get up about four in the morning before they've all flown back, make a huge pile of wood, set it alight, then chuck sulphur onto the fire. That sulphur smoke sticks to the leaves and the friggin bats can't cop it. The only problem is if you do it too close to where you reside, you'll never get that sulphur smell out, long as you live.

Grim was restless and wanted a long walk, so I joined him and we strode out through the neat suburban streets, through the mining accommodations, sky criss-crossed with grey falcons and black kites. Tiny yellow butterflies as yellow as butter fluttering everywhere. Black-eyed Susan, glory lily, poinciana (pronounced locally as Poncey Anna), swamp foxtail. Up Towers Hill amongst the red and grey boulders and the pussy tail grass were Chinee apple trees. We did not talk as we took in the long vista to the western sky at dusk, a strip of gold low down, fitting for Gold Town, then a swatch of deep lavender, and above it vestiges of pale blue growing paler as the sun set. We could see the movements of horses and buggies and pedestrians in the city centre. Off to one side was the Proving Ground, the site behind one of the bottom pubs where most nights there was loud betting on fistfights. This was a puncher's town.

The Northern Miner, Charters Towers, 13 December 1909
BOXING. REGAN V. GRIM
(By 'Cestus.')
Daylight fighting, until quite recently, was as dead as bell-bottomed trousers, but following in the footsteps of Americans, our pugilists have adopted the idea, and have gone back to the old, old fashioned sunlight wherein to do battle, and snare the almighty dollar. Charters Towers, following the lead, put on its first daylight fight on Saturday afternoon at the Olympia Rink,[96] Paddy Regan and Joe Grim being the contestants.

The ring was situated on the concrete floor, the smooth surface being matted with linoleum, while sand was spread immediately outside the ropes. Ample seating accommodation had been provided, and the novelty of the daylight drew many new faces to the ringside.

Grim was the first in the ring, and standing in his corner started an oration. 'Well gentlemen,' he said, 'there has been so much kick about the money here, and I have good rep. in America, and here, and I am willing for the winner to take all.'

Regan came in, and white with excitement, stepped up close to Grim, and lifting up his voice, told the audience that they all knew that he had paid Grim's fare here, and as he had signed for a 60 per cent and 40 per cent division, he will have to hold to that.

'I'll fight when he complies with these articles.' Warming to his work, he went on to say, 'Look here, I'm giving away two stone, and if he wants to fight so willing, and eager, give the money to Mr. Currie, and we'll fight, only it must be 60 and 40.'

The excitement of the financial situation extended to the audience, who voiced advice with that easy benevolence for which it is noted, 'Never mind, Paddy, go for the lot' or 'Quite right, Paddy, make him stick to the articles.' 'Here, Skiter, go and speak to Regan.' Skiter wheeled snappily and growled, 'You might just as well talk to an iron pot as talk to him.'

---

96 An indoor skating hall at the corner of Bow and Mary Streets.

The deadlock hung on, and the crowd, fearing to miss the fight, kept urging the men on. 'Never mind the money, fix it after,' until at last, a matter of fact genius, with fine authority, ordered 'Hat' Currie 'to go and get the dough.' Nothing loth, 'Hat' went, and Regan, evidently thinking it might be too heavy, accompanied him.

A long delay followed, until the five shilling seats began to ask where Regan was, and their blood ran cold as a voice said, 'He's gone home; he did that on Saturday night;' but it was not so, for immediately the green trunks were seen coming through the ropes, and the crowd settled itself contentedly.

Grim's weight was given as 12–4, and Regan, with a sly grin, said his was 11–4. Personally I should say Grim went about 13–4 and Regan 12 stone. There was £78 in the house. Mr. J. Benham refereed the fight, and Mr. Aaronson kept the time.

At the start Regan was tense with excitement, and he opened carefully but later warmed up and fought well. His left was always in Grimm's face, and the Italian-American mopped them up as a sponge absorbs water.

His face puffed a bit at the finish, especially his left cheek, and his nose bled freely, but otherwise he seemed to be adamant. It was not an interesting fight, for Grim was apparently dead out of condition. He was fat, and as slow as a hippopotamus.

He has no defence and very little aggression, though when he does cut loose he hits very hard. In the second round he caught Regan a wallop on the back of the head, which knocked him onto his knees. It was a wild smash, but it landed, and shook Regan to his toes. He went down all right, and as Grim came in, grabbed him by the ankles. Grim's seconds called foul, but Referee Benham took no notice, for it was obvious that Regan was completely rattled and his clutch at Grim was as instinct as that of a drowning man.

The audience were mad with excitement, some wanting a foul, the others wanting a fight, and as Grim's seconds were insistent Benham said he would get out of the ring. Grim spoke up and said, 'I don't want to win on a foul, all I want is to fight.' Regan had got on his feet, and as Grim rushed and whirled into him the Northern heavyweight seemed unable to stall him off. Around the ring they went, Grim's wild rushes causing yells of laughter, but Regan weathered through, and came up cooler than before, and from that out shaped like a tradesman and won all along the line.

Regan's fouling of Grim in the second round may have been excusable enough, but later on, although he had insisted on clean break regulating the fight, he deliberately held with one hand and hit with the other. It was right outside all fair punching, and he deserved to lose the fight. Grim, eventually angered and outraged, retaliated, and though the referee did more than his best to see the fight conducted fairly, stray punches were sent in right through the fight, Regan being the most persistent offender. The Italian fought like a man, albeit a slow one. 'All I want, gentlemen, is a fair deal,' he said, and it seems a pity that Regan, who was leading all along, should have seen fit to depart from the rules of the game.

The referee had warned Regan in the first and second rounds, and no bearmaster ever had more anxiety or rightdown hard work than our erstwhile prominent forward. His shirt was covered with vermillion splashes, his pants were torn from the knee down in regular directoire style, but good sport that he is, he kept going, and like our own Bill, 'did his best.'

Taken right through, the fight was not a spectacular one, as no one likes to see a game man knocked about, and Grim's condition would not allow of his taking too many liberties. To win he needs must keep rushing, and in that mops up no end of heavy cracks when up against a fighter like Regan, who is a fine hitter. Grim only needs to land one uppercut in the right place to win, but his delivery is so slow, that unless his man is bustled off his feet, there is not too much chance. There is some talk of the pair meeting later, and though Regan will score up innumerable points, there is always the chance of Grim getting there, and so the fight is sure to draw well.

The fight went the full 20 rounds, Regan winning on points.

There was plenty of comedy during the fight. Grim is somewhat of a character, and under Regan's fighting mug, there lurks an Irish humour. At the bell Regan would often hold up his arms wide, 'with a both hands free' sort of air. Grim would mimic the attitude, or mooch to his corner not deigning to take any notice. In one round Regan was paying particular attention to Grim's body, and after a hard rally Grim stepped back, and sticking out his all too ample 'tummy,' smacked it with his open glove, calling out in his soft Italian voice, 'Didn't you see him hit me here,' then blowing his nose coolly, he went into the fighting line.

Toward the conclusion of the fight Regan grew confident and commenced taunting Grim's seconds, 'What about the big mug now,' he said. The onlookers thought he meant Grim, but the remark really referred to himself, for Grim's supporters had so designated him. Barring his hitting when holding, Regan fought a good battle, and there is no doubt that the decision was a fair and sensible one.

If the boxing ring is an altar it is not an altar of sacrifice solely but one of consecration and redemption. Sometimes.

Joyce Carol Oates, *On Boxing*

49.

My uncle had stopped speaking. He seemed to be asleep. His eyes were closed. I crept up the makeshift staircase of books to the top of the towering east bank, and gently covered him with some dusty periodicals, and removed the empty sherry flagon, and let him be. My uncle did not stir. I slid down the mound of books, a tottering wave destined to never quite break, and locked the door behind me, and slipped into a world where the sky had grown soft and dark and it was a perfect time for wandering home.

50.

My uncle, who was not my uncle, into the silence:

Red of split eye. Red of fist-tattooed ribs. Red of swollen cheek. Red of misting blood. Red of courage. Red of stupidity. Red the orb that now won't stop glowing, throbbing somewhere perpetual and impossible inside the skull. Red of the red dirt desert interior. Red of the sunset over Claremont. Red of the plunging velvet stage curtain in the Gaiety Theatre, Zeehan. Red of Jack Johnson's laughing maw. Red of the coals in the campfire by the Burdekin. Red of the long red day that stretches from the start of life and crosses the span, short or long, and ends at the point of end. And red, possibly, beyond that. We do not know.

51.

I have fought in better rings, and fought before better houses. A daytime crowd at a skating rink in Charters Towers is not exactly the National Ath Club in Philly, with four bands[97] leading my singing countrymen through the streets to watch me perform, spectators hanging from the rafters, and my name chanted like an incantation. I am tired, and I am damaged, but they will get the full Joe Grim show, including the finishing headspring. There has been much chivvying about money; my opponent claims that he is the draw card, and stubbornly declined every side bet that I could go the distance. And yet somehow I found the patience not to care; I knew that it would take as long as it took. And now he is in the fight, a smug sort of man, fast with his left and nimble on his feet but not Jack Johnson, not George Cole, not Jim Scanlan or Dixie Kid or Sailor Burke. In the second he leaned in a while too long and I clubbed him behind the ear and I thought it might all be over, and that put me off-kilter. While he writhed on the mat, Regan wrapped his arm around my lead leg like a child clinging to its mother on the first day of school. I declined the foul, and was much more comfortable when the barrage resumed. He has sliced

---

97 *Los Angeles Herald*, 15 September 1909. 'Grim … this queer specimen of the unusual in the fighting game … No gamer or pluckier man ever stepped in to the ring. It was only his bulldog tenacity of purpose to remain the limit which enabled him to hold out. Not for a moment would he seek quarter, and although he was beaten almost to a pulp on many occasions he would not permit his seconds to stop a bout to save him from punishment. The night of his fight with Jack Johnson at the National A. C. is an event which will be remembered by all the fighting fans of the city. Over five thousand enthusiastic Italians, accompanied by four brass bands, paraded downtown … '

me a little, hit me hard once over the heart, is content to bang from a distance and look good for his local followers. It's okay.

The sunlight this far north has special clarity and ferocity and it comes at a slant through the slightly grubby windows and I can see every face at ringside as clearly as I can see my own gloves. A distracting novelty. There is my faithful follower, the worry-faced child-man, unblinking and glib, mouth falling open oftentimes as if to speak but staying mute, unable to look and unable to look away. Beside him for a time was Saitchell, watching the younger man with paternal interest. I saw him lean and say something, then he got up with one hand resting on the acolyte's shoulder, pushed through the scattered seating, and made his way out through an open door into the platinum daylight. And then I noticed the goat standing in that open door, watching proceedings with benign disdain, and beside the goat was another goat who looked fetchingly at our goat, and I hoped that this might be bringing our goat happiness. (I strained my cauliflowered ears and clearly heard the goat say to his companion, 'There are two types of people in this world: those who can extrapolate from incomplete data.' The second goat waggled its whiskery chin and said, 'Oh now, goat, I really do delight in your comic stylings.')

Ticking through the rounds, tired and flat now, throwing the lead uppercut occasionally to push Regan back, then clinching, and holding my gloves up and rocking side to side, just entering into the covenant, receiving the sacrament of hard leather, proffering my face for benediction by blows, easing my mind the longer the ordeal goes. We have settled on twenty stanzas. It is an appropriately exhausting distance. We'll get there. Meanwhile I treasure each and every round.

Sincere thanks to Belinda Byrne, Jo Canham, Karen Ferguson, Peter Long, John Rawlings, the Rensing Center, Tom Reynolds, Martin Shaw, Ben Walter, Alana Wilcox, Will Rees, Ed Wright, and Crystal Sikma. And, of course, to the enigmatic Joe Grim who surpassed all.

Michael Winkler is a writer based in Melbourne, living on the
unceded lands of the Wurundjeri people of the Kulin nation.
He has a serviceable left rip and a jaw of surpassing delicacy.
michaelwinkler.com.au

Typeset in Minion, Bureau Grotesque, and Knockout.

Printed at the Coach House on bpNichol Lane in Toronto, Ontario, on Zephyr Antique Laid paper, which was manufactured, acid-free, in Saint-Jérôme, Quebec, from second-growth forests. This book was printed with vegetable-based ink on a 1973 Heidelberg KORD offset litho press. Its pages were folded on a Baumfolder, gathered by hand, bound on a Sulby Auto-Minabinda, and trimmed on a Polar single-knife cutter.

Coach House is on the traditional territory of many nations, including the Mississaugas of the Credit, the Anishnabeg, the Chippewa, the Haudenosaunee, and the Wendat peoples, and is now home to many diverse First Nations, Inuit, and Métis peoples. We acknowledge that Toronto is covered by Treaty 13 with the Mississaugas of the Credit. We are grateful to live and work on this land.

Seen through the press by Alana Wilcox
Interior design by Crystal Sikma
Author photo by Joe Winkler

Coach House Books
80 bpNichol Lane
Toronto ON M5S 3J4
Canada

416 979 2217
800 367 6360

mail@chbooks.com
www.chbooks.com